SENSEI'S STORIES

TALES OF TWO MASTERS

BY JUSTIN D. PANZA

For my family
who has made me strong.

私を強くしてくれた
私の家族のために。

"We live together.
   We fight together.
      We die together.

   We all might as well get along."

—MASTER TIEN

「一緒に住います。
　一緒に戦います。
　　一緒に死にます。

　一緒に仲良くしましょう。」

　　　ティエン先生

CONTENTS

序文
一人多岐

PREFACE

ONE OF MANY BRANCHES

It is funny to imagine a *dojo* where a single master roams the halls every day, every month, every year of a school's existence. Much like in the stories that follow, I used to envision a wise sage with a Yoda-like quality who speaks in short quotes of pertinence and constantly sports a critical eye. A master of masters with the power to tear you down with a flick of their wrist and the ability to impart wisdom in but a few short words.

Though my conception of this old character, who has been made famous by countless authors and actors, sounds like quite the formidable figure, many of these qualities appeared in the teachers I have had over the years, each one endowed with a unique spirit brought out when they took command of the mat. It was clear how they each came from a common chord, like a thread that spindles out as a web of benevolence and knowledge. I believe this is one of the most essential qualities that made the *dojo* I first started in such an empowering place to train.

I will forever hold my teachers dear; their presence in my life was unquestionably transformational. I simply see each student's transformation as an unprovoked passing of pure power and goodness from one martial generation to the next.

Now, my colleagues and I see hundreds of students each week, so we are regularly reminded of how much of an influence we make in their lives.

We as instructors are, without a doubt, a source of inspiration, wisdom and joy. Therefore, what we say, what we do and how we behave truly matter. It has been my hope that with each class I teach, I am able to keep the lessons of my teachers fervent and meaningful, so one day, my old students will be able to say, "I remember when you taught me [blank] and I still carry that with me today."

∽

The five stories contained in this volume each explore a different virtue, tenet, or struggle I have confronted or combatted with in my time training. Each is prominent, recurring, and critical to the development of the martial artists I have trained with. Though each story naturally contains scenes of adrenaline-pumping combat, that should not be the focus of your attention. The focus should be on uncovering each of the five virtues and how they all play a role in the character's continuing journey toward personal perfection. As it is with any and every technique and strategy I ever study, they are devices in constant states of refinement.

So, whether or not you, the reader, are a martial artist who regularly jumps onto the mat to test your skills and physical prowess, these five virtues still bleed into everything we do, inside and outside of the *dojo*.

In reading these stories, I give you the mission of seeking out these five virtues in your own lives. Analyze them, and apply them. See for yourself how they can enhance your own quality of life. In doing so, you too can pass on the wisdom of the warrior to those who matter to you.

Enjoy!

プロローグ　嵐

THE STORM

I sit on the large, smooth granite stone struggling to keep my eyes closed. The sound around me plays its enticing melody. The stream beneath me flows so gracefully, so elegantly, it does all it can tempting me to gaze upon it.

A loud *snap* in my mind, and I remember what my mission is.

Stay focused.

I repeat this to myself. *Stay focused.*

Of all the things I've ever trained, meditation has always been the hardest. How could someone ask me to take my mind off something I took value in *enjoying*? It's like trying to take car keys away from a professional driver or a brush away from a painter. You don't do it!

But still I sit… I rest my hands in my lap and try to let the sound of the stream relax my excited mind.

How will your mind ever truly see if you allow it to focus on other things? The voice of my *sensei* whispers in my mind. *How will you ever hear to the fullest truth if you are always speaking?* He often spoke as though he were a cryptic puzzle.

But still I sit… With my sleeves rolled up, I can feel the breeze gliding over the hairs of my naked arms and tickling the whiskers of my unshaven chin.

The place where I sit is far removed from the bustling city, which after fifteen years is finally becoming this grand commercial marvel. *Sensei* told me that because of the influences of Western modernization, the old ways are becoming far removed from our daily habits. During our training, he always pressed upon me that the lineage heads are responsible for preserving the tradition of the ancestors who came before.

"But shouldn't the lineage adapt with the times?" I questioned. "Bring the old in with the new? If the art you are responsible for is truly timeless, should we not let it evolve?"

To which I was scolded for thinking such a thought. It wasn't my place to give decrees on the future of the lineage.

It only makes sense, I assured myself. *For what else do we study the art? For what else do we train? This isn't for amusement; this is for self-mastery.*

But still I sit… pondering those questions in a different way. *For what else do I study? For what else do I train?*

The clouds ease their way between the sun and myself. They cast a grey shade over the trees and shrubs, in bloom at the peak of their season, radiating a sweet aroma that inundates my nostrils.

Then a harsh clap of thunder echoes from far off in the distance. *My time on this stone might be nearing its end.*

But still I sit... Two birds in their nest above me signal to their comrades of the impending storm. It doesn't take long for them all to convene. By their ceaseless banter and heavy dispositions, they make it apparent that they are not going to flee. They know their nest is strong. They know that *they* are strong. This storm is *nothing* to them. They had learned as much from their ancestors, who themselves had tried their hand at their own strongholds and withstood maelstroms and forces mightier than themselves.

We are like the birds, I suddenly think.

The thought resonates from the back of my mind. I suppose... maybe... it is because I listened, as *sensei* had told me those many years ago. I simply listened.

Flash!! Clap!! The thunder rattles my skull just after a vicious white glimmer pierces through my still-closed eyelids. I hear droplets meeting the leaves above me. They begin to patter atop my hands, which still rest gently in my lap.

The deities are bidding me leave from their forest, and yet, under the nest of the brave birds, I do not heed them. For my insolence, they send a torrent down upon me, forcing the stream to rise while throwing the gusts against the leaves.

But still I sit... With the birds, undeterred.

But still I sit...

—

邪
悪
な
先
生

THE MALEVOLENT SENSEI

Each of the short and spirited children jumped as high as they could, but, even still, the soft foam *bo* struck their feet. From the other end of the foreboding weapon boomed a loud voice. "Get your knees up high! As high as your heart!" the *sensei* shouted through his pruned lips. "Jump like the monkey that leaps between the branches."

He swung again for the students' feet. This time, they lifted their knees just like he suggested, and each child passed over the staff without losing a limb.

"Better. Much better," he announced with a grin, still aiming his trusty weapon right at them. "Now, one last test: dodge the staff before it strikes you in the head."

"How do we do that?" blurted the newest student,

a shaggy-haired seven-year-old who stood a little taller than the rest.

"Imagine your body is like a door being opened by a gentle breeze." The child tilted his head in bewilderment. "Try it." The *sensei* flipped the long staff high overhead. The whole class watched as it arced through the air over their circle and fell toward the student's head.

The shaggy-haired boy, with his hands out wide, looked up to see the great black staff soaring down. His muscles twitched, itching for action, and just as his mind thought to make a move…

Bop!!

The staff hit loudly atop his head.

"Ouch!" he muttered.

The *sensei* slid the staff back through his hands and stood it up by his side. "What happened?" he asked inquisitively.

"I got hit!" replied the pouting student. He crossed his arms and flared his shoulders.

The *sensei* looked the boy in his honey brown eyes. Even though he was clearly flustered, the *sensei* noticed a fire burning inside of him.

The *sensei* looked around to the rest of his students. Six other young *ninja* lined the circle atop the red and green *tatami* mats. He asked them, "When it comes to dodging, what do we always say?"

Together they shouted, "Move your feet!"

"Exactly. Always move your feet." He readied the staff in his hands once more. "Erica," he said, looking to the shorter girl who stood next to the livid boy, "Show Tony how you do it." He tossed the staff up overhead again, aiming for Erica's unguarded noggin. Just as the staff was inches from her head, she stepped to the side and spun her body like a door, getting out of the way just enough to feel the air rush along her face and course through her curly blonde hair. The weapon crashed down to the mat below.

"Well done, well done!" tittered the grey-haired *sensei*. "Tony, are you ready for another try?"

Tony still had his eyes on Erica. He had watched every motion she made, observed exactly when she had made her move. He turned back to the *sensei* and answered, "Bring it on!" This time, Tony's voice was filled with unwavering confidence. He sunk down lower and stared at the staff that was braced in the *sensei's* hands.

The master sunk down, too, gripping the mat with his *tabi*-covered toes. He squeezed the foam staff even tighter. His eyes stared Tony down.

Tony looked up from the staff and locked eyes with the old man, not an ounce shaken by the master's testing attempt to jar his spirit.

Then, with their eyes still locked, the *sensei* chucked the back end of the staff over again, flinging it faster than any time before. *Tony will never get out of the way*, the others thought.

But Tony thought something very, very different. *Piece of cake.*

He stepped to the side and turned his body sharply, finding the ground and bracing it in time for the foam staff to fall right in front of him and crash to the floor in front of his toes with the loudest *thud!!* Tony, even after dodging the staff, still had his eyes glued on his teacher. He flashed him his proud, partly toothless smile.

The genial *sensei* smiled back, showing off his partly toothless smile, too.

∽

The *sensei* huddled the seven students together and sat them in a circle beneath the *kamidana*. Each of them knelt and rested their hands atop of their knees in *seiza*.

The *sensei* also sat in *seiza* in front of them. He looked down at the young faces, each of them looking back up with glimpses of wonder hoping for the next words from the *sensei* to be more "cool" knowledge about the "old-timey" *ninja* of "ancient" Japan. *Sensei* knew they were suckers for good stories.

"Someone tell me something good about a teacher you have in your life."

Some of the smiles vanished when they heard the question, but one student, a rotund boy, promptly threw his hand up.

"James."

"They are funny."

"How are they funny?"

"They make me laugh."

The *sensei* squinted and flattened his mouth, but noticing his own uncouth reaction, he brought his focus back to the child. "Okay, okay. How do they make you laugh?"

"They always tell a joke while they teach."

"But if your teacher is always making jokes, are you still learning anything?"

"Yeah." Little James nodded assertively. "You do that all the time."

The *sensei* chuckled. "I guess I do." He looked back around the circle. "Anything else? What else does a good teacher do?"

The *sensei* saw another hand go up out of the corner of his eye. He looked to his right at a petite brunette who wore a pink neon shirt underneath her clean white *gi* top. "Anna."

"They try and try to make you learn it," she said in a sweetly meek voice.

"Why do they try so hard?"

"Because..." She thought for a moment, having trouble finding her words. "Because they want you to learn it."

"Do you think, if they are trying so hard to make you learn it, they are being bossy?"

"No!" she shouted, shaking her head fervently. "They want you to learn because they care. They care about you."

With a strong finger pointing at her, the *sensei* replied, "Bingo! I believe *that* is a great trait in a teacher. I do not think someone is a very good teacher if they do not care about their students. It is not just what the student learns that matters, after all. It is also about how they learn it. Very important."

The *sensei* looked up and checked the time on a red maple framed clock on the wall. Its numerals were written in Japanese *kanji*.

I can spare a few moments more, he thought. Then, he

looked back down at his enraptured students.

"Here's a story to teach you the importance of having a good teacher."

"Yes," sounded a few of the boys. Several of the girls shushed them with an upraised finger over their lips.

Once the noise trailed off, the *sensei* began.

『昔々...』

A *sensei* is a not only a descendant in the lineage of a martial art, but is another martial artist's guide on a special kind of journey. A *sensei* steers his or her student toward a long-term goal. Sometimes, however, the wrong *sensei* can steer a student far off course.

There was once a boy who visited his *sensei's dojo* twice a week every week for three years. The *sensei* watched the boy grow up to become a strong young man in just that short time. He had taught him many things: how to leap over the tallest castle wall, how to snap the end of a spear with a single kick.

The boy was ever grateful for all the time his *sensei* invested in him and for all the wisdom he imparted.

But there came a day when the young man felt that his aging *sensei* was running out of things to share. The *sensei's* usual challenges were becoming too easy. Trying to be courteous, the student held back his true power to make his *sensei* believe there was something more he could teach him, but after several weeks, the student grew tired of holding himself back.

He left his teacher's *dojo* one evening and decided to take a stroll through town. He slyly walked by other schools along the eerie avenue, being extra cautious no one would see him. He would stand for several moments in front of each *dojo*, peek through the windows, and spy on the students training inside. He saw groups of students striking with all their might, twirling their weapons faster than he could imagine. *Their* sensei *must have the skills I am trying to attain for myself.*

Each day after training, the student would pass by one particular *dojo* on his way from his *sensei's* and watch their classes through the tall iron gates. One day, a voice came from around the corner of the gate. "If you are so interested, why not come in and try for yourself?"

The student skipped back from the gate, his heart racing.

"You pass by here every few days. I see you spying from the mat, staring at us."

"I have another *sensei*, and I enjoy training with him. I would never leave him."

The man quizzed him with his narrow stare. "And yet something else draws your eye. There's nothing wrong with that." There was an unsettling tone in his voice. "What if I taught you, one on one? After my regular classes finish, and after yours? Let's train together. No one must know. You're just trying to become the best martial artist you can be. So am I. So are my students."

The teacher had just given the unwitting student an offer he couldn't refuse: a chance to train harder, learn more, and still preserve the faith of his *sensei*.

Without hesitation, he answered, "Okay. When should we begin?"

"Two weeks from tonight. Meet me here after all my students have left. But leave your old uniform behind. No other regalia is permitted inside my school."

The student gave a reverent bow to the man, then ran for his home bearing a huge smile. He was delighted for what he was about to learn and excited at the prospect of how much more he was going to grow.

∽

Two weeks went by slowly for the student, who counted down the days to begin his new training.

After the student gathered his belongings, he said goodbye to his *sensei* and dashed out of the *dojo*. He rushed down the dark streets until he made it to the other school. With the sky pitch black and the building nearly empty, the only person there other than himself was the school's head instructor, the man who gave the student his golden invitation, Kurogawa.

The training was rough; Kurogawa did not hold back. He said there was no time for silly forms or striking on targets. He said they would never help in a real fight. All that mattered was the combat.

For any misstep the student made, Kurogawa reprimanded him. The student left his *dojo* after each lesson bruised and aching but still thrilled with what he was learning. He could already sense his own improvement.

"Don't mind these marks, boy," Kurogawa told him. "They are merely a testament to how much stronger you are becoming. At this rate, even *you* will be able to defeat your old *sensei* one day."

Kurogawa always found a way to remind the student of his *sensei* and place him in some disparaging light. The student would play along, laughing at the cruel jokes and barbarous jabs, but deep down, he felt pained to be sneaking around behind his *sensei's* back, training with some other teacher, one with less sensibilities toward his student.

∽

After several more weeks, the routine had become a ritual: train with *sensei*, head down the road, train with Kurogawa, go home. But, without warning, Kurogawa began inviting other students into their lessons, some new to the school and some who had trained with Kurogawa for years. What was originally an arrangement for private training with Kurogawa became less like lessons and more like matches.

Each successive session, sparring became more and more vicious. Some days, the student would try to sideline himself after a veteran student struck him too hard, to which Kurogawa would push him back onto the mat and shout, "In a real fight, you can't just quit because you get hit! Suck it up and continue!"

When the beatings became more than the student was comfortable with, he asked Kurogawa if he could at least strap on some padding. Kurogawa responded unfavorably to his request, scolding him further, demeaning him, and forcing him to do push-ups for even asking such a stupid question, all the while the other students practiced their kicks against his ribs.

But, still, each late-night session ended the same: with Kurogawa offering him verses of encouragement reinforcing how much stronger he was becoming and how much closer to mastery he was getting. It was odd that the words sounded so familiar to him. "These are trials meant to test your spirit. Your challenge is to push through them." What Kurogawa told him kept his spirits up and gave him the strength to walk back home through the ghastly hours of the night.

∽

In training the next afternoon with his *sensei*, the student's movements were noticeably off; they did not look or feel as crisp as they usually were. The injuries from his late-night scrimmages were hindering him. His *sensei* approached and asked what was ailing him, to which the student replied, "Nothing. I'll do better."

His *sensei* wore a forlorn expression. "I know you will. You always find a way to out-match yourself. I'm thankful to have a student like you. You possess a spirit that strives for perfection. You're a true treasure." The student beamed when he heard this. For a moment, they shared a joint satisfaction, but as *sensei* turned away, the student's face dropped to an anguished pout. *If* sensei *knew the truth, he'd surely take back his words.*

∽

The student walked slowly down the dark avenue to Kurogawa's *dojo* and stopped before the large iron gates. He watched as the last students from the final class left the small building and brushed by him, rubbing their sores and massaging their twinges but chatting joyously to themselves. They repeated back to each other what Kurogawa had recited to them:

"You'll go far if you keep training with me... You'll be stronger than any other student I've taught... Keep coming back and you'll only go up, up to the top..."

The student stood there a moment, looking on at the empty space, as he battled his conscience. Amid the ramblings in his head, a formidable voice called out to him. "What are you doing just standing out there? We're wasting time. Come in," Kurogawa commanded.

"I think—" the student started, stumbling to find the right words to express his feelings without angering the teacher further. "I think I'm going to rest for today."

"Rest is for the weak, boy. You won't get any better sitting at home. Let's move it."

The student felt compelled to move forward, as though puppet strings tugged at his muscles, commanding him to move. Like a child toward his parent, he felt unable to disappoint Kurogawa. He took a shaky step passed the threshold of the iron gate, but was quickly halted by a gentle hand that gripped at his shoulder.

"A true warrior knows when to back down. I taught you that." The voice behind him sounded older, creakier and all too familiar. He turned his head to see his *sensei* with a cold look piercing Kurogawa.

"*Sensei*. I'm sorry. I—"

"You don't have to explain. I've known for a while you've been training with Kurogawa."

"You knew?! How—"

"He told me so himself." The young man felt his stomach turn. "He came to me the morning after your first session to boast about your raw talent, and to rub it in my face how he would turn you into the fighter I could not. Kurogawa has a nasty side to him. You must have sensed it. That is why he left me many years ago."

"Wait, *sensei*. You mean… Kurogawa—"

"Is my former student. My first student." The boy couldn't believe his ears. "He wasn't satisfied with his progress while under my guidance, and so he left to pursue other feats. After some time, he opened his own school close to my own hoping that he could prove himself superior to me.

"I knew when he first started he was a bad apple. He always had a dark look in his eye, and the path he took matched it, a path of loathing and the need to feel dominant. I am ashamed of myself I didn't do more to change him.

"It taught me never to give up on any student because the future can either be a thing of brilliance… or a heavy menace.

"Somewhere along the way, he grew a smooth tongue; he gets a hold of other students, fills their heads with skewed aspirations, completely steering them from the true Way—"

"Quit feeding my student your lies, old man," Kurogawa interrupted. "He's my treasure."

The student's ear burned when he heard the word. He felt a heavy air press down upon him. It made sense now why he still felt compelled to keep returning to Kurogawa. All the wisdom, all the kind words… they were the same words from *sensei* himself. That was why Kurogawa felt so familiar at times. He knew now that he was just another blind individual drawn in by a teacher whose vocation was to mold a machine rather than aid a human in their own self-growth.

The realization stirred up something in the student. A new confidence. A new conviction. "*Sensei*, let me make this up to you by showing you what I've learned."

"You're going to challenge me?" Kurogawa scoffed.

"I'm going to honor my real *sensei*, the one who actually believes in me, who treats me respectfully, who acknowledges the person I am, not just my skill so he can mold it into what he wants," the student proclaimed.

"I'll be at your side. You don't have to hold back anymore," *sensei* asserted. He squeezed his student's shoulder again, pumping through him all the confidence he needed to win.

『…終 』

The kids' mouths gaped open. They held their breath for quite a while until one blurted out, "Then what happened??" The tension had mounted. They were on the edge of their seats.

"You'll have to find out next time," the *sensei* replied, sneaking a glance up at the maple *kanji* clock, "We are already five minutes passed. Your parents probably don't want this old man blabbering on all evening. Off with you. Get home, study hard, rest up."

He bowed forward from his seated pose, resting his hands on the *tatami* mat beneath him. The children copied along, not as gracefully but respectfully nonetheless.

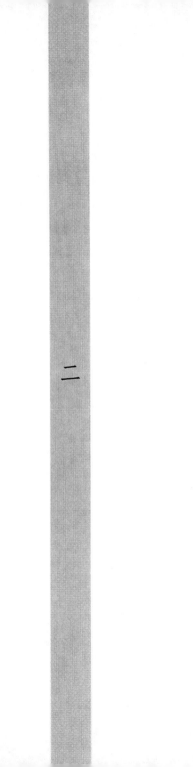

弱
体
化
分
隊

The Unraveling Squad

———————

You'll never move it if you all keep tugging at dif-ferent times," called Julia, a tall, dark-haired teen-ager, one of the *dojo's* junior instructors. She watched from the edge of the mat as a group of youth students tried to move one of the heavy punching bags off to the side.

"You keep pushing it in the wrong direction!" shouted one of the boys to another.

"I'm not! You are!" he retorted.

"I'm doing all the work," chimed in the third.

Julia smacked her forehead as she watched the three argue over who was doing a worse job. "Guys, you've got to work together."

"I'm trying but—"

"I'm trying but—"

"I'm trying but—"

Each of the three rattled off a different excuse for why his teammates were making their seemingly simple task more of a hassle.

Julia just shook her head. "With that attitude," she responded, "you'll never get it done. Come on, guys."

Hearing the commotion, the *sensei* ambled out from his office and looked on at the mat. The three boys were tugging and wrestling with the heavy bag, making more of a spectacle out of their situation than coming any closer to a solution, let alone an accord.

He walked up next to Julia. "Having a hard time getting them to cooperate?"

"Yep," Julia said exasperatingly.

"You've got to get them on the same page," her *sensei* advised.

"How do I do that? They keep throwing in their own opinions, but not one of them listens to the other."

"Hmm," the *sensei* pondered. "Gather them in."

Julia looked at him and took note of her teacher's assured face, a look she commonly saw. Julia then looked out at the mat, where the herd of youth were still buzzing around moving their gear to assemble their course. "Attention!!" she bellowed. Her voice bounced off the high wooden walls. The cluster of wily kids froze and turned their heads toward Julia. "*Sensei* said to huddle in."

A few cheers rang out as the sounds of kicking targets and crash pads fell to the floor. The kids rushed over to *sensei*, some taking a knee, others sitting straight to their bottoms.

Sensei crouched down, facing them all. "Teamwork is one of the most valuable skills of a martial artist. Without good teamwork, missions fail. Back in the days of the *ninja*, solid teamwork meant the difference between life and death for an entire clan."

In an instant, the room fell deafeningly silent.

『昔々... 』

There are three levels within a network of *ninja*: the *jōnin*, the *chūnin*, and the *genin*. The *jōnin* sit at the top and decide if a mission is worth the time, manpower and safety of their clansmen. The *chūnin* sit in the middle and delegate their teams, assign them their duties and relay to them all the pertinent information they need for their assignment. The *genin* at the bottom are the field agents, the ones who get the job done, capturing the glory by putting themselves right in the middle of the danger.

A legend has been passed down through the *ninja* families for generations meant to teach *genin* the importance of working as a team; without the other members, the likelihood of a mission's success was slim, and the repercussions for failing were severe: capture, torture and death were always looming possibilities.

There were once three *ninja* named Taro, Jiro and Saburo, all skilled in different areas and said to be the best from their respective clans. One day, they were assembled by a *chūnin* and tasked with a critical mission: the daughter of a *daimyō* had been taken by *samurai* from a neighboring region and needed to be brought back home.

These *samurai* desired neither money nor fame; their desire was to insight a war.

The *daimyō* from the province implored his military consort to devise a way to get his daughter back without creating any political discord between the rival territories, so the consort sought out his clandestine contact, a *chūnin* from a *ninja* family living in secret within the territory.

After reviewing the situation carefully, the *jōnin* commander granted his *chūnin* permission to aid the *daimyō*, and with that, the *chūnin* assembled his ace unit.

So, the three unacquainted ninja set out to find the *daimyō's* daughter.

∽

It took two days before the *ninja* could determine the enemy's location. They found them hiding away on a mountain on the border of the two regions. The enemy had set up camp tucked away in a little opening of a lush forest.

"The daughter could be in any of these tents," said Saburo, the youngest of the three. "We should devise a plan to scout out the camp—"

"There's an easy solution to this," interjected Taro, the oldest. "I'll scare them out all at once." Before his comrades could get another word from their mouths, he weaved his fingers together in a fluid assortment of signs. Then, in a puff of smoke, he transformed into a tiger.

If I take out all the bandits, I can end this all now.

The tiger paraded its way to the front of the enemy's camp. The first *samurai* to see the tiger let out a scream and promptly called for help; his comrades rushed out of their tents, carrying chains and ropes with weights hooked to each end. They twirled their weapons high overhead then threw them at the tiger.

The orange tiger leapt this way and that, avoiding the weights and chains and ropes, but after a few successful dodges, its luck ran out as one of the ropes bound up its front leg. The tiger struggled to shake its leg free. It jostled the man on the other end who yanked back harder in response. Amid the struggle, a cold grey chain affixed itself to one of the tiger's back legs, then two more ropes tied themselves around its body. The tiger was immobilized in the center of the camp.

"Wily, brave beast, you thought you had us."

The *ninja's* plan to scare the enemies out had failed, leaving him trapped among his many adversaries.

"They caught him. They caught Taro," Jiro muttered, his lips quivering. "I have to rescue him. I have to save him. There's no time to wait."

"Jiro, hold on!" Saburo exclaimed. "We need to do this together—"

Jiro was too quick. He weaved his hands together in rapid

succession, and in a puff of smoke, transformed into a scaly green snake, hissing madly. Saburo watched as the snake slithered up the path into the camp.

It moved elegantly between the many tents, peeking its head under each of the flaps, searching for Taro the tiger.

As it slipped its head under one particular tent, it saw a man dressed in the finest armor of all the other *samurai*. From his attire and his poise, he looked to be the leader responsible for the taking of the *daimyō's* daughter. He was sitting at a table, writing on a scroll.

If I take out the leader, I can end this all now.

The snake slithered closer, wrapped itself around the leg of the table, and moved its way up to the top. It hid itself among the many things resting on the surface: a long thin candle, a deep inkwell, a stack of documents.

After several moments of watching its enemy, the snake felt that it was time to strike. It waited for the scribbling hand to bring itself nearer. The snake opened its mouth, bearing its two long fangs. Ready to move, it sprang forward, hissing fervently as it lunged for the still-scoring hand, but midway through its leap, everything went black.

The snake sunk its teeth into the first thing it felt, discovering quickly that it was not flesh but the wall of a ceramic drinking vessel. The snake bussed around wildly in the darkness, no exit to be found.

"Cunning little serpent. You thought you had me."

Minutes later, the snake found itself falling from its dark vessel into a glass jar beside a giant tiger bound in chains.

"We'll have some fun with you both later," the commander said. He picked up a black lid and sealed the top shut.

Saburo looked on from his hiding spot. His two reckless teammates had rushed into the camp without a plan, completely ignoring each of the others. Taro, with an ego the size of the tiger he became, rushed in proudly, hoping to make short work of the assignment. Jiro, bursting with panic, rushed in frantically without using sense or strategy. Now they were both trapped, just like the *daimyō's* daughter, wherever she may have been.

"I'll never be able to rescue the *daimyō's* daughter all on my own. I need Taro and Jiro at my side." Saburo pinched his eyes shut, considering everything up until now. He thought about the enemy, how many were inside each tent. He thought about their weaponry, how most of them used ropes and chains. He thought about the tents, how they were arranged and where they could be keeping Taro and Jiro captive.

Saburo knew he would have to be inconspicuous, so he weaved his hands together, and from a puff of smoke emerged a simple, ordinary butterfly that fluttered its way into the camp.

If I can meet up with my comrades, we can end this all now.

The butterfly moved about in all directions passing over some of the foes, who didn't bother to even register the butterfly in their midst.

With its red wings, it landed on a crate of rations some ways from the front of the camp. Its beady eyes scanned around but could not pin down its friends.

"Did you hear about the tiger that wandered into camp earlier?" asked one of the men to his comrade.

"I did," the other replied. "Did you hear about the snake that snuck into the commander's tent and nearly bit him?"

"No!"

"I heard he caught it bare-handed."

"Two creatures, one after the other. Unbelievable."

"They said they are holding them both in the back of the camp."

"I can understand keeping a tiger, but why not just kill the snake?"

"Commander says he wants to pit it against the tiger and see which one outlasts the other."

The two men chuckled as they continued on their way just out of earshot.

The butterfly flapped its dainty wings and flew farther down the camp, passing only a few more enemy *samurai*. It came to an opening where, to its luck, it found its friends, confined and removed from the closest set of tents.

The butterfly landed just in front of the lethargic tiger, which was still exhausted from its earlier struggle. The tiger opened its eyes to see the butterfly disappear in a puff of smoke and be replaced by its comrade, Saburo, back in his human form.

Saburo scanned the binding chains and saw the lock that kept them together. *I'll need my teammate for this. He can pick a lock quicker than I can.* He looked to the side of the tiger and saw the glass jar that held his slippery second teammate. He reached down and took off the thick black lid, then turned the jar on its side to let his comrade slither out with ease. The snake, too, transformed; Jiro had returned.

"Thank you," Jiro said solemnly to Saburo. "I'm glad you found us."

"Don't worry about it." Saburo replied. "Let's free Taro, then save the *daimyō's* daughter."

Jiro nodded. He reached inside his satchel and pulled out a set of metal picks, then set to work at the lock that kept the tiger's chains together. Saburo scuttled to the nearest tent several meters away and peeked around its edge, looking out for any enemies. He saw the two men from before were making their way over.

Click! "I got it," Jiro called. He unfastened the lock from the chain links. Saburo dashed back over to Jiro and the tiger. Together, the two men began unraveling the chains. They tried to be quick but had to pace themselves else the rattling chains would give them away.

"What was that noise?" said a voice from the other side of the nearest tent.

The tiger found it hard to keep still. It whined and jittered its legs, trying to shake the chains off.

"Take it easy, Taro," Saburo whispered into the tiger's ear.

"We've almost finished," Jiro said, trying to help reassure his entangled comrade.

After less than a minute, the chains fell off and the tiger was free. Quickly, the tiger transformed, and there stood Taro, reunited with his teammates.

"Go *shush* that beast!" came another voice.

"Follow me," Saburo said to the others. He weaved his hands at a speed that Taro and Jiro could copy along. The three had transformed into a trio of butterflies, their wings the colors of scarlet red, ocean blue and emerald green. They fluttered together and over the tents, following Saburo in formation.

As they rose higher into the air, they saw that one of the *samurai* below made it to the clearing to find the knocked over jar and the empty chains.

"Oh no!" he cried. "The tiger is gone! The snake, too!"

The three butterflies then saw more of the men below running around in chaos, squawking at one another.

"There's a tiger on the loose!"

"I think the snake is venomous!"

Well above the chaos, the three butterflies glided on the breeze waiting for any sign that would lead them to the *daimyō's* daughter.

"We have to move the girl!" shouted the commander from below. He pushed his way through the tent flaps.

Another *samurai* approached the commander with a young girl in tow. She was immaculately dressed but caked in dirt and sweat. Her wrists were bound by chains much like the ones that had kept the tiger at bay.

The commander took the girl from his minion, getting a firm grip on her arm. He escorted her along, shouting, "Get walking and don't stop!"

The butterflies hovered over the scene, then dove down like speeding falcons. They vanished in another cloud of smoke only to reappear as their human selves, crashing down atop the commander, knocking him to the ground.

Saburo reached his arm under the girl's, much gentler than

the commander had before. He told her in an assuring tone, "Have no fear. We're here to get you back home."

Assuaged as she was, the girl's face bore an expression of disbelief. *Where did these three come from,* she thought. *Popping out of thin air. Incredible.*

Before she could get a word out, she noticed that the tallest one had changed shape. No longer was a man standing there, but instead a white tiger, staring down the enemies who were rushing at them with their weapons brandished firmly in their menacing hands. As they approached, the tiger swung its mighty paw at the fronts of the long weapons, knocking them right out of their grips.

Jiro leapt onto the tiger's back and sprang up as high as he could, changing shape in midair into a small monkey. It ran up, down and around each of the men, got to their hands and proceeded to bite and scratch and punch them until they dropped their weapons.

"The tiger will make a path," Saburo said. The girl turned her head back to him. "Stay behind it, no matter what. I promise, we will get you out of here."

"Thank you," she said through her shallow breath.

After seeing the monkey get all the men to drop their weapons, the tiger charged forward, enticing the unarmed herd of bandits to scatter to the sides. Saburo and the girl ran behind it. The monkey leapt from the ground to the back of the tiger, where it transformed back into Jiro, who reached into his satchel once more and pulled out a hook and rope.

He swung his tool down to the ground, hooked the head of

a lone spear and yanked it up to himself. Jiro was ready to make sure no one stood in their path.

If we push through these men, we can end this all now.

"Saburo, we won't make you both run behind," Jiro shouted back. "Hoist her up here."

Saburo heeded his comrade. He grabbed the girl around her waist and hoisted her up, draping her along the tiger's back. Sitting up, she straddled her legs around its body. Saburo then reached down and grabbed one of the enemy's fallen swords. He gripped the handle firmly, ready to swing.

The three *ninja* hustled passed the remaining *samurai*. As more men tried to intercept them, each *ninja* did what they needed to do to keep the girl safe. Taro the tiger bounded over the ones in front. Jiro thrust at enemies to the right. Saburo fended off those to the left.

Without trouble, the three *ninja* crossed the threshold of the camp with their charge, dashing through the trees and out of sight, safely setting a course for home.

『...終 』

No one can do everything all on their own. A little bit of effort from everyone working as a team can accomplish great things." The *sensei* looked to the boys, "You three: go move that bag again. Together."

Everyone stood up and spread back out to finish their tasks. Julia and the *sensei* watched the three boys get a firm grip on the heavy bag once more. The boy in front called back to them,

"On three. One… two… three!"

They heaved the bag at once and noted instantly how the heaviness had magically dissolved. The bag glided along the mat with ease. After several more heaves, the bag was back in its proper spot.

The *sensei* smiled upon the three who high-fived each other in solidarity.

Julia leaned over and whispered into his ear, "You don't think that one might have been overkill, *sensei*?"

The *sensei* shrugged. "Best to share with them a lesson worth remembering."

三

忍者の完璧な実習

THE NINJA'S PERFECT PRACTICE

L et's try it again," the *sensei* exclaimed to his student. He was a burly man in his thirties, passionate but characteristically impatient. *Sensei* could tell that even though he was a beginner, he had the craving to gain as much material as he could.

"Let's move on, *sensei*. I think I'm getting it. I can practice this one later," proclaimed the student. They had only been practicing the technique for five minutes.

The student was doing a decent job performing the motions of the technique, all the gestures and steps, but what he lacked was the *gokui*, the 'essence.'

That is the point of the lesson, thought the *sensei*, *that's what I want to transmit to him*, but this hard-headed pupil wasn't mature enough to see that yet.

"It's your lesson time," *sensei* replied with a groan.

"Okay, what's next?" asked the student, clearly not sensing the *sensei's* frustration.

"I have one more technique for you. It will likely take the remainder of this lesson, and still, I query you won't have mastered it even weeks after this."

"Let me see it," the student asked with a twinkle in his eye. "I love a challenge."

The *sensei* held back his irritation. "Walk over to that punching bag." The student did so. "Ball up your fist." The student did so. "Now punch."

The student paused. He pondered for a moment. *A punch*, thought the student. *Easy*. He reared back his fist and thrust it forward. It collided with the bag, pressing the cushion inward several inches. The student pulled his fist back, gleaming at the result. He looked over to the *sensei*, who stood there with a scowl. "Wrong. Do it again."

Wrong! The student's face dropped. He had just dented the bag. *If it had been an actual person, it would have been devastating.* He gave the *sensei* a darting look of confusion.

"Do it again," the *sensei* repeated, his hands folded behind his back.

The student clinched his fist again. He reared it back, then struck the bag. It dented again, just the same as before, but this time, the student felt a slight ache in his knuckle. He pulled his hand back and shook it a little, letting his knuckles loosen.

"Do it again," *sensei* asserted.

"*Sensei,*" the student started, but he was firmly interrupted.

"You want to learn a new technique or not?" *Sensei* cleverly played to the man's desires.

The student still didn't understand where his teacher was going with this. He reared back and struck again. The same pain roared through his hand this time. He let out a *yelp*. "*Sensei*, you keep making me punch. You see I'm in pain."

"Let every action be a lesson. Every move you make tells you something, first like a whisper, then like a roar. You will never learn a thing from only a few fervent attempts. Why do you think mastery, true mastery, takes decades?"

The student did not know. He shook his head, yearning for the answer.

"The first few years are rife with mistakes. We learn from those mistakes, and then begin to grow. My *sensei* once told me a teacher is merely someone who has made more mistakes than his students have ever attempted, and if we never learn from them, we can never grow in our endeavor."

The student braced his hand and pressed into his swelling knuckles, ears still fixed upon his *sensei's* sage words.

『昔々...』

A student, whom we shall call Chi, stood in the courtyard of the martial academy, lifting his leg and kicking a stump bound in taut rope. He repeated this action over and over. Sweat poured from his head. Once time was up, he switched his feet and began to kick with the new side, striking in a steady rhythm. *If I strike once every second and keep that pace, that's*

*3,600 kicks. I know I'll slow down, and my rhythm will break,
but I won't stop. That's the important thing: I won't stop.*

A voice rang in his ear as he kicked. *No one is proficient
until they've done it 10,000 times.* "10,000 is easy," the student
asserted.

"Take a break, why don't yah?" said Chi's fellow classmate.
He looked over his shoulder, still kicking, and saw Sui standing
there, arms folded in front of his chest. "What's the point in
training one move so much? It's not like a simple stomp kick
will beat the enemy."

"Better to have a move that works than a hundred that fail."

"Really? If that's how you see it, care to make a wager?"

Chi stopped his kick, eager to hear the proposal. "What do
you have in mind?" he asked through his panting breath. Beads
of sweat dripped from his nose and chin to the ground below.

"You pick one technique. Just one. Train it rigorously, day
and night if you must. I'll train fifty old moves and fifty new.
And come the end of the month, we'll spar. Using only our
learned tools. We'll see who is right."

Chi smiled. "Deal," he responded without a second thought.
He reached out his hand for a shake.

Sui unfolded his arms, reached out his hand as well, and
grasped Chi's firmly. "Good luck."

ᔆ

The challenge was set for the end of the month; the boys
had twenty-two days to prepare. On top of their regular train-

ing with their teachers, the two spent extra time before and after learning all they could.

As Sui made a list of the techniques he knew, he contemplated the moves he didn't. *What if I find myself in that position?* He jotted these questions down as well.

Chi, on the other hand, went to the meditation garden, plopped himself atop a mossy stone, and began to concentrate. *One move to beat all others,* he pondered. *Hmm, this is trickier than I thought.* Chi sat atop the mossy rock for several hours. Occasionally, he would look around the garden, not knowing what he was looking for, but hoping that whatever caught his eye would illuminate the slightest hint of inspiration.

Then, he took his hands and set them behind his back onto the cold hard stone below. He looked back behind him, rubbing his hands on the stony surface. Then a sound caught his attention. He looked down to see the water flowing at the base of the stone, moving around the obstruction. That was it. That was what Chi needed.

Chi sought out the help of his teachers, and asked them whatever he could related to his chosen technique. They offered him suggestions, insights, and philosophies, all of which Chi took into consideration and adapted into his training.

Sui spent several days consulting the senior students whom, over their many more years at the school, amassed a plethora of techniques Sui couldn't even imagine. He asked them to show him the moves, which they generously did. Sui received the technique, then tried it on the senior student. When he felt he had grasped it, he bowed to them, giving his thanks, then

rushed back to his room and wrote down the technique from
memory.

Sui's collection had grown exponentially over the first few
days. Pages and pages of notes and instructions inundated his
journal. He spent the last hour before lights out each night reviewing the pages of notes. Sometimes, he would leap from his
bed and go through the motions to assure himself he had them
down pat.

∽

With the challenge only five more days away, Chi and Sui
were using every spare moment they had to prepare. When Sui
reached out to the last of the students, he went back to the ones
he had previously seen, prodding them for any more moves
they might have forgotten. Though the students walked him
through some steps that trickled from the backs of their minds,
they warned him that they were not entirely sure about them,
but Sui took note of them anyway.

Chi asked three of his favorite training partners to help him
out. "The challenge is a few days away, and I need to test out
my technique against a lot of others. Think of anything you can,
and come at me with it. We will see if it works."

So, for two hours, the four boys drilled and drilled and
drilled together. Chi reproduced his technique against punches
and grabs and kicks and more. For every defense that did not
feel right, they tried again until there was no doubt Chi could
defeat the attack. His confidence grew as large as Sui's book of

notes.

The challenge was soon to commence.

∽

A hoard of students made their way to the courtyard to witness the challenge. Both Chi and Sui, over the past twenty-two days, had conspired with many people throughout the school, students and teachers alike, each of whom took a profound interest in the upcoming contest, so as was their nature, they spread the word to their friends and colleagues, inciting only more interest in the spectacle. And so, the courtyard had filled with onlookers who circled the two classmates.

Chi and Sui stood at opposite ends, looking at each other, not in a menacing way, but in a way that boasted their individual self-assurance. Sui had recruited one of the senior-most students to be the officiator.

"The rules are simple. The match is over when one fighter concedes. Sui is permitted the use of one hundred techniques, outlined officially on this document." He raised a thick, bound-up scroll over his head. "Chi is permitted the use of one technique of his choosing, which he will demonstrate at the start of the match. In true *ninja* fashion, neither party knows the other's register of techniques." He then lowered his voice, slating Chi subtly, "or lack thereof."

Chi didn't flinch. He took a hefty breath in, then blew it right back out. His muscles were loose, ready to go.

"On my mark, you may begin." The officiator shoved Sui's

scroll back into the lining of his *gi* top, then raised both of his hands high in the air. The courtyard fell silent, except for the auspicious breeze that blew through the anxious crowd. "*Hajime!*"

The crowd suddenly erupted in cheer from their pent-up excitement. Twenty-two days finally behind them, it was time to watch the result of the two boy's strenuous labor.

Chi gripped the ground with his talon-like toes, his *tabi* shoes firming his grip.

Sui bent his knees, then rocked forward to the balls of his feet, as though about to pounce.

Chi was ready.

Sui lunged forward, closing the gap between them as his legs kicked him along the courtyard floor. It seemed as though not even a second had gone by, and Sui was within striking range of Chi.

Sui reared his arm back, clenched his fist and punched for the side of Chi's face.

Chi, catching wind of Sui's move, lifted his arm up, creating a wall, hiding his head behind it.

Sui's inner arm crashed into Chi's, ricocheting off with force that Sui had never conceived of before. He caught his footing, dust kicking up madly around his feet. He looked back at Chi, who was standing there in the same stance they both had learned since the day they first started training, but never had he experienced the level of potency that came from the ricochet.

Sui's arm was screaming. "So that's your move?" he declared. "A simple block? Interesting choice."

Many of the students in the crowd began to murmur amongst themselves. They whispered such things as:

"He's given away his technique."

"Sui will never let him use that again."

"Chi is done for."

The teachers in the crowd all looked over the students, listening to their quick opinions. They smirked to one another. They had, after all, advised Chi when he came to them with his idea. They were now curious as to if and how he might pull off this victory.

Sui was finished tending to his wounded arm. His focus was clear again on the objective. *I shouldn't try to punch him, but what if I use it as a ruse?* Sui plotted, then made his move. He leapt forward again, coming in with another strike to Chi's head.

Again, Chi lifted his arm, ready to intercept.

Sui, however, opened his palm mid-strike and made his fist into the shape of a sword. He let it strike into Chi's forearm, hoping to weaken it and deter Chi from using it again.

To Sui's surprise, his strike didn't move Chi in the slightest. "What in the world?" he uttered, jumping away.

"You should have conditioned your fist a little more, Sui. Then your strike might have done some good. I've hardened my forearms to withstand direct attacks, so trying to barrel down on them will be tough. What's your next move? I'm ready."

Sui snarled. "I've got plenty more to show you, Chi. Just keep that arm up where I can see it."

Chi rotated his hand and waved Sui on.

Fueled by a livid fire in his chest, Sui charged forward, knowing he was going to have to break Chi's defense down. He came in with a massive flurry of punches and kicks, moving from every direction, trying to keep Chi off guard.

The eyes of one of the students in the crowd lit up when she recognized Sui's pattern of movement. She took note of the intricacies with which he was moving his limbs to attack, but she knew something was missing from it all.

Chi moved rather gracefully, bringing his arms in the path of the oncoming assaults, thwarting each and every one.

Sui broke off again, catching his breath.

"That's what's off. He has the combinations, and makes them look effortless, but he hasn't conditioned them yet," the senior student whispered to her teacher. "He's quick, but he can't deliver the power behind the hits."

"Exactly," the teacher asserted.

Sui gritted his teeth, all the contact points on his limbs were growing tender. *Striking isn't the answer*, he weighed. *Time to tear him down, then.* Sui approached Chi, knowing he couldn't strike back, as per the conditions of the challenge, so he threw a feint punch to get Chi to block it, and pulled it when Chi's arm lifted to intercept.

Hurriedly, he rushed to wrap his arms around Chi's, then jerked his own arms to move Chi's like a lever. *Surely, he'll concede if I threaten to dislocate his shoulder joint.*

Once again, try as he might, Chi's arm was immovable. Sui, like a monkey eyeing an unfamiliar object, tugged and heaved this way and that, but the unyielding arm remained frozen in the air. Sui, in his tumultuous stupor, peered at Chi, who wore nothing but a smirk that only aggravated him even more.

He ditched this attempt, and pranced around behind him. *Can't block if I'm behind you, can you?* Sui flung one of his arms around widely, about to secure it around Chi's neck.

Recognizing this, Chi brought his arm up between his neck and Sui's gangly, bruising arm. Sui began to tighten down, squeezing as hard as he could, but after several seconds, he discerned that Chi was still standing, not unconscious as he intended. It was then that he realized Chi was blocking his choke; his wrist left a small space for his airway, utterly foiling the advanced maneuver.

Sui, enraged, tried anyway to squeeze it all together. *I'll just choke you with your own arm!* He huffed and puffed and strained to no avail. So, Sui let him go, stepped back, and composed himself.

The murmurs amongst the students continued:

"He can't be punched."

"He can't be kicked."

"He can't be broken."

"He can't be choked."

Sui, try as he might, pushed the voices from his mind, needing to gather himself and decide his next move.

Chi, undeterred, finally spoke. "I am like stone. You are like water. Anything you try will just bounce off me. All one hundred techniques: I will crush them all."

"Shut up!!" snarled Sui, charging in, uncontrollably. Out of frustration, he went for a punch, knowing Chi would just block it, but the tension had reached its boiling point. Sui needed to let it out.

Brush! Pass! Slam!!

Chi slipped to the inside of the punch, gliding along the surface of the dirt beneath him. Sui's punch continued cruising to where Chi's face *had* been, but along the way, Sui realized his arm was wedging away, his face becoming more and more open, more vulnerable.

Just as quickly as he threw his fruitless attack, he lost his balance, stumbled forward and fell right into Chi's open hand.

Sui's feet flew ahead of him faster than his body could possibly keep up. The impact was so intense, color left Sui's vision for a moment. He crashed to the ground, landing flat on his back.

Chi stood over him, looking down to see if he was all right.

Huff. Puff. "I concede, Chi," Sui proclaimed in a soft, weakened voice. "You were right."

Graciously, Chi reached his arm down, meeting hands with Sui's. Peace instantly flowed between them once more. Then, Chi hoisted Sui to his feet.

"Chi is the winner!" shouted the officiator. He grabbed Chi by his free hand and held it up high. The students in the crowd cheered. The uproar echoed throughout the courtyard. Even the teachers stood in amazement at Chi's feat.

Sui, amid the outrageous clamor, leaned his head in and spoke into Chi's ear. "How did you do it? I don't understand."

"Patience, observance, asking questions. Looking at *one* thing from *every* angle. Finding its values, testing its limitations. Then embodying it so it works as a part of me."

Sui was aghast. "Please, show me how to do that."

"Tomorrow. Tomorrow, I'll show you. It'll start with a simple block. And we'll have to do it ten thousand times."

『...終 』

The *sensei's* student had taken a knee sometime during his telling of the story. He looked up to his teacher avidly.

"There's no such thing as a simple block, or a simple punch. Think of all the things Chi learned from performing his technique ten thousand times. How much stronger all around he became. I hope that from this lesson you've learned one thing: see all aspects to everything. There's far more to a punch than just punching."

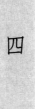

四

The Legend of Unshakable Tien

不動なティエンの伝説

"Do you need me to grab you another tea, *sensei*?" whispered Bill.

The old man turned his head up to him. "Yes, please."

As Bill left the table, Mr. Stewart, a business man dressed head to toe in a black suit, charcoal tie, and round, onyx cuff links, began speaking again. "If you implemented the marketing program and POS system with its rewards and benefits, we expect your net profit to exceed a 15% increase by next August, and certainly a 30% increase by January."

"Certainly," muttered the *sensei*, looking away from Mr. Stewart.

Bill had returned, passing the cup of tea along the table and fitting it into *sensei's* hand.

"*Arigatō.*"

"This is all presuming your school makes the necessary changes we already outlined in the modification plan." Mr. Stewart set his fingertips down atop the stack of stapled papers and eased it closer to *sensei*, who brought his gaze down to it reproachfully. Catching the sensation from the old man's eyes, Mr. Stewart continued, "This is not a decision you have to make right now. Take all this, think it over. I'll get back in touch with you all in, say, two weeks," he looked around at the three men across from him.

"Absolutely," replied Owen. "We appreciate all you've done. Really." He scanned the table with all the documents. "We will look it over and have our answer the next time we talk."

Mr. Stewart smiled congenially, then rose from the table, grabbing his tall cup of coffee. Owen watched as the man traipsed away and out the door. Bill was still watching his *sensei*, whose eyes hadn't lifted from the documents.

"This is not what the martial arts are about," he uttered glumly. He shuffled the documents around looking at their charts, graphs and text, then brought his hand to the cup of tea, embracing the vessel to soak up its warmth. "When I started our school, I admit, I had visions of it housing hundreds of passionate students, everyone willing to open their minds to understanding the Way. None of it had to do with money, with 'business practice.'"

"But these are the times we live in, *sensei*," Bill explained. "If you hope to attract any students these days, you have to start online. People don't just seek things out anymore. They don't know *what* they want. You have to *show* them what they want."

"That sounds ridiculous," *sensei* scoffed.

Owen leaned in a little. "Think about what good this will do for the school, though. New equipment, a stronger air conditioning unit. These little luxuries will encourage more people to want to train. No one wants to train in a humid hell box."

"Then they shouldn't train with me," he retorted grumpily.

"*Sensei*, I know how badly you want to keep the old ways around, but listen to what we are saying. People want innovation. They are attracted to the shiny stuff that catches their eyes."

"That's just it, Owen. That's not the kind of person I want to train. I don't want to be the man on the street with a dancing monkey in my window to get customers to come into my school. I don't want to have to *lure in* potential students. If they do not know what it is they want, what it is they need, they are not ready to begin their training. Not with me, at least."

"We are looking out for the well-being of the school, *sensei*. If we don't get new students, we… you… will lose your building. It won't matter anymore *who* comes through your doors because you won't *have* any." Owen suddenly frowned. "I don't wish to come across as crass, but that's the reality, *sensei*."

"I know, I know. I'm just… riled at this situation. I need to get out of here. Clear my head for a while."

"Is there anything you need us to do?" asked Bill.

"No, no. Enjoy your afternoon. I'll see you both later for classes."

"*Hai*," they both responded in unison.

Sensei got up from the table, grasping his cup. He lifted it to his lips and threw back the last drops of tea into his mouth. Just as quickly, he brought it back down, walked over to the recycle bin and threw it inside. He passed through the coffee shop doors indignantly, shoving his hands into his pants pockets, lowering his head and setting forth into the bustling streets, eager to leave the arena where he felt he was trapped in a losing battle.

∽

The grey-haired man closed the office door behind him after flipping a switch on the wall. The overhead lights flickered on, revealing a treasure trove of memorabilia scattered throughout the tiny cube-shaped room.

Adorning the walls were dozens of framed black and white portraits of students standing together wearing ruddy white *gi* uniforms and various colored *obi*. Some of the scenes took place atop hardwood floors with students moving defiantly throughout the room, weapons in hand. Others took place outside in a grove with a sun so bright the image itself was almost bleach white. The commonality between every photo was the smile worn on each face in frame.

Sensei scanned the snapshots along the wall, smiling to himself.

Turning around and looking down, he set his fingertips onto his desk, and as he stepped around behind it, he ran his fingers along the hardwood top. Where his colleagues' desks were teeming with assorted documents and instructional books, *sensei's* desk was nearly vacant save for a small reading lamp, a ceramic pot holding pens and pencils, a tower candle on a slate grey saucer, a red ink pad, and a *hanko* stamp with his name carved into its bottom.

Sensei sat in a small, black swivel chair, then flicked the switch on the power cord of the desk lamp. Instantly, the image of *samurai* in the heat of battle revealed itself on the paper screens that housed the bulb. It cast the scene onto the surrounding walls, overlapping the antique framed photographs. The *sensei* scanned the war scene of imperial guards with their legs knee-deep in a river and their swords locked together in a heated assault.

He reached for the handle of his desk drawer, and opened it. Glimmering in the light was a leather-bound journal. He reached in, carefully placing it within his hand, admiring its soft textured feel. It was the color of sea foam, crafted with the image of "The Great Wave Off Kanagawa." He set it atop his desk, unwound the thin leather tie that sealed it shut, then opened the cover. On the first page, boldly written in black calligraphy, were the words:

不動 な ティエンの伝説
The Legend of Unshakable Tien

Beneath this line was another set of *kanji* written in a more original script. It was the name of the author of the journal.

And beneath that was inscribed the date the entry was formally written:

昭和三十七年吉日

This auspicious day in 1962

Sensei flipped to the next page and saw the vertically in-scribed foreign characters lining the face of the page. They were scored so neatly and legibly that *sensei*, even with his old eyes, could read them effortlessly at a steady pace. As he perused the lines, he eased back into his swivel chair, letting his muscles give way to the back cushion. His mind started to forget the floresc-cent light overhead, or the *samurai* desk lamp beside him. All that possessed his attention were the well-written words.

『昔々...』

How I met the great Tien was far unlike any other casual meeting.

I was being chased, you see, by some typical thugs. At the time, I was but a simple kid of only fourteen years, innocent, virtuous, and being hunted down by the lowest of the low. They wanted to pilfer what little I had, which was only enough to get me across the river on that beautiful Sunday afternoon.

As I ran, I panted and wheezed and struggled to see, the sunlight and sweat stinging my eyes. I tried not to stop. I tried to pretend I wasn't tiring.

But then I stopped, and I tired.

I was grabbing at my knees and sucking air. The footsteps

of the thugs beat along the ground behind me, kicking up dust in their wake. I looked over my shoulder and saw the four of them, their faces bruised and scarred, their fists lined with dirt and scabs. I was not ready to be turned to pulp.

The four brutes stepped closer, striking their palms with their own fists. I could hear their knuckles crack on impact. They were warming them up... for me.

By then, I turned fully around to face them taking in each of their faces to memory. Though I didn't *desire* to undergo this terrible event, I wanted to remember it. I wanted to remind myself well after it was over that this was just another experience. It was *my* experience. Nothing could change that. Nothing should stop me from remembering every gruesome detail.

I closed my eyes and took a final breath in, ready to let the four go to work. *It will all be over soon,* I kept repeating to myself.

Thwop! Thwop! Thwop! The sound of pummeling filled my ears, but, to my surprise, I was unmoved. I was still intact. I opened my eyes quickly to see why this was so.

Before me stood a boy my age with tangled dark hair, bandages wrapped all the way up both his arms, shorts that revealed his bruised lower legs, and a beat-up, sleeveless, shredded cotton undershirt. He stood there resolutely, staring down the fourth thug across from him, who himself was gazing down at his cronies, all sprawled out along the ground squeezing their bleeding noses and patting their injured ribs.

"Who the hell are you?" spat the fourth thug.

"The Devil of the Northern Valley. Call me Tien."

The thug let out an uncontrollable cackle. "'Devil of the Northern Valley?' Your village already give you some slick nickname?" He howled again, clasping his cramping gut, but somewhere between chortles, he went silent as Devil Tien, having leapt forward like a panther, laid a kick right to his mouth, knocking in several of his teeth and sending the crude man flying back off his feet.

I looked on at the scene, completely awestruck. The boy, who could only be a few months older than me at the most, stood so strongly; he didn't even show, as far as I could tell, a hint of fear in him.

Without turning back to look at me, he asked, "Are you okay? They didn't hurt you, did they?"

I shook my head, "I'm fine, thanks." My wonder had to be quite apparent. "How did you—"

"You better get out of here before they come to."

"What? I—"

"You're fortunate I was passing through."

Tien, if that really was his name, squatted down low, setting his hand to the ground.

"Hold on! Let me come with you."

"Why?" He peered over his shoulder with a confused and jarring gaze as though it were the strangest thing he had ever been asked.

"I'm a writer." Tien turned at the sound of my fumbling through my well-fastened satchel. I grabbed my journal from within and thrust it forward so he could get a clear view. "You see?" Its green leather binding reflected in the draping sunlight.

"If you'll let me, I'd like to write about your adventures."

"My life isn't anything anyone else would want to read about."

I dawned a disbelieving expression. "You just took down four men empty-handed. You're not some ordinary kid."

"You'd get in the way of my training."

"Believe me, I won't get in your way. I care more than a shred about keeping myself intact."

"No thanks," he said, sounding irritated now.

"Just think about it for a minute," I asserted, outstretching my hand to him like I was reaching to hold him down. "Let me record your tales. Even if not for the public, let me write them for you."

Tien looked a little incensed. He could tell I wasn't letting up. After an awkward lull, he opened his mouth and uttered airily, "Fine. Whatever. But one condition: if you can't keep up, don't expect me to wait on you." And just like that, not holding for any cheer of gratitude, Tien ascended straight up into the air, vanishing among the tree branches.

I stood there, my mouth gaping open again in disbelief as I watched him bound from tree to tree like some monkey king. Then, just as quickly, I noticed how far ahead he had gotten, so I rushed off after him. I could not afford to lose him.

∽

I sat on the stone by the water, watching him as he worked. With his legs kicked up in the air, he proceeded to push himself up by the tips of his fingers. His balance and strength were inspiring. When he finished several repetitions, he left the pose with a front handspring, landing evenly on his feet. Then he grabbed a stick from the ground and began to twirl it in various exotic patterns over his head and around his torso, sometimes punching the tip of each end to act out a strike to some invisible foe.

"How long have you been doing this? Coming out here and training?"

Tien finished a head-level strike, eyes still piercing the ethereal opponent. "A long time," he answered sternly, trying not to strain his focus.

"…Ah," was all I could muster in response. He obviously didn't feel like talking, but the questions I had for him kept flooding my mind, and as they reached the point that they were hitting the brim, my mouth opened and spat out, "Where's your master?"

Tien chucked the stick out of his hands. It landed in a bushel of tall grass, where several bugs fluttered out hastily into the humid air.

After a strange, stale pause, Tien changed the subject. "Let's get food," he uttered, maybe not saying it directly to me, but more or less at me or toward me or, I didn't know, honestly. I immediately felt like those bugs in the grass: in his presence but of no real consequence to him.

We sat down in the booth in the noodle shop. Steam emanating from the cooking station behind the bar trailed around us. The sounds of pots and ladles clanging around masked the lingering tenseness that enveloped our table.

"Thanks again," I said, not knowing why I felt the need to say it.

Hmph. He grumbled, casting a look away from me.

Then something inside my gut reeled around. I burst up out of my seat, slammed my hands on the table and yelled, "What's wrong with you?! What's with your foul attitude? You save my butt, I try to thank you, you shake it off, completely ignore me! You act like me and everyone else don't even exist. I'm trying to get to know you, I'm trying to show you I genuinely care, but you keep shrugging me off!"

I had half a mind to grab him by his soggy shirt and heave him up to eye level and keep telling him off, but I still had sense enough to know that would have been a mistake, so after the few seconds when he didn't make an effort to reply, I sat back down and looked away, still fuming.

"My family came here from China when I was three years old." I shot my eyes over to him, astounded he even spoke a word. "When I was seven, our home was looted by the local gang. They took everything. They beat my parents to a pulp. My two older brothers had to quit school to help them replenish their savings. We had nothing to live off of.

"I'll never understand why, but when my brothers couldn't find good work, they turned to working for the gang that did this to us. Whoever their leader was gave them little assignments, like laundering contraband or delivering stolen merchandise to vendors.

"Not long after, they got in deeper. When they realized just how lucrative their work was, they kept the money for themselves. My parents and I didn't see much of them anymore.

"When the higher-ups decided to use my brothers in a more 'permanent capacity,' they were told to return home and wipe us out. They had to rid themselves of any family ties to show their loyalty to their new family.

"My mother and father locked me in my room to keep me safe, but their cries rang through the walls and filled my head, no matter how hard I pressed my hands to my ears to tune them out.

"Several minutes went by; I took my hands from my ears, wiped my eyes, and listened to the silence... until my oldest brother stomped the door down.

"They looked down at me, their teary-eyed little brother. They did what they did. But they *didn't* finish me off. Out of my swollen eyes, I looked up at them, and for the briefest moment, as clear as anything I'd ever seen, I saw a tear running down their cheeks. Then everything went black.

"I spent several years in an orphanage with nothing but that awful memory and this hateful attitude. While I was there, I got to train with a martial artist who visited every few days to teach some of us. With every lesson, I vowed to get stronger so that no one could ever hurt me again.

"When I was ten, the newspapers said my brothers were dead. The gang dumped their bodies in the river. It was strange, though; I wasn't sad.

"I have no place I call home. I've wandered around the country since, trying to find masters who will train me for a while, then I leave. I feel weird staying attached to any place for too long."

It took me a moment to realize: this wasn't a story about a fighter trying to get stronger. This was a story about a vengeful young man who lost his family. If I continued to follow him, I dared not guess where it would take me.

∽

He didn't like that I had written his story in my journal. He snatched the book from my hands and tore the page clean out. "How dare you! That's not your story to keep!"

"Tien—"

"Why do you write all this anyway? What good is it to you?"

"These are my experiences, Tien. I treasure them."

He threw the journal back at me. It hit me in the chest before it fell down into my hands. The front flap fell open, revealing the torn section from which he now vigorously waved the pages. "This one is mine. You can't have it." He crumpled it into a ball, then shoved it into his pocket.

"Tien, I don't think you understand."

"Understand what," he muttered, folding his arms callously.

I closed the cover and stood up. "You never even asked about my past, you self-centered—" I was genuinely at a loss for the right word.

But Tien was still a little taken aback. I could tell because his chest had hollowed and his brow curled down. "Enlighten me."

"I lost my parents too!"

He didn't seem moved by this.

"Not just my parents. My grandparents, my aunts, uncles, cousins. They're all gone!"

Tien finally began to show some sign of anxiety.

"I've only ever lived on a trading ship. My whole family traveled across the sea and along the coasts bartering with townsfolk from different ports. The Chinese navy mistook our ship for a pirate vessel they had been hunting. They sunk our ship with cannon fire. I was the only one who survived, perched on a large crate for two days before I washed ashore. Everything I ever knew, everyone I ever loved, was sunk into the sea."

"...I'm sorry," Tien proclaimed, his voice soft.

"...Yeah." There was a silence between us that seemed to last forever. My heart was busting for the first time in a long time. "I can't just leave that in my past. That's why I write things down. They are all part of the experience. Wherever I am in my life, I can go back and review my past, see where I've grown, discover how I've changed. None of us should stay the same. That's not what living is for. I can go back to any period and revisit my former self. Maybe I'll find a lesson in the past I didn't get before. Who knows? But ignoring your past, running from it, holds *no* value."

The next morning at breakfast was a far different affair than the night before. Tien asked more about my past and also opened up about his life before his wandering quest. It was during those exchanges we came across the subject of his future plans, how one day he wanted to open a school of his own, one that welcomed all travelers. "I know I'll have to find a *sensei* first."

"Then go find a *sensei*. Commit to training with him or her for as long as it takes."

"What will you do?"

"Isn't it obvious? I'm more suited for the arts. I'll go apprentice under a great writer. Let's meet up in two years' time. We'll share of our adventures, and see if our paths are still leading us toward our goals."

∽

And so, it went. Over the next ten years, we arranged to meet every other year in the same place. We shared of our adventures, detailed our exploits, and gossiped about our teachers.

Tien shared of tales about a wayward student in his *sensei's* past, how he tried to lure Tien himself into training with him; how one teacher sent him and his fellows on dangerous assignments that tested their skills when their life really was on the line; how he bested a rival of his in an unlikely competition of mastery; and how one of his teachers was a master of the *bokken* and how she never once lost a match against a live blade.

I shared with him my travels with my teacher throughout the country, learning all I could about literature and storytelling, telling the story of a people within the confines of only a few short pages.

Our tales were audacious wonders in their own right, and each visit we had, our stories became more grandiose and thrilling.

On our fifth reunion, we sat down once more and revisited our long-awaited aspirations. We both learned we had become adept enough in our skills; we no longer needed a master by our side. Together, we would open a *dojo* in the city. I would write of our students' exploits, to encourage others to come study under Tien's tutelage.

It would be a calm life, one driven by experience, as I had always hoped for. Our experiences would be the foothold for the shining futures of students for the coming decades.

∽

As with any school, the first years were rather slow, but the few students we had were the most eager of all: learned, humble. We could trust them to lead some of the classes as Tien and I explored our arts further. My first compendium of stories became a top seller, I'm proud to boast. It explored the wanderings of a young boy from China questing for a legendary treasure.

∽

The real trouble came in the tenth year. We were both on hiatus from our travels, conducting several special classes each week. I had students interested in the literary arts. Tien had martial artists from other styles coming in curious about what he was sharing.

There was one evening on a Saturday where more than thirty students from another school all barged into our *dojo*. I'll never forget the sight of them: wearing their black and red *gi*, their foreheads wrapped with a band emblazoned with the name of their school.

"Bring forward your Chinese scum!" cried the leader of the pack who stood several paces ahead of all the others. He had his hands on his waist, his chin up high, peering around with a callous smirk. All of Tien's students gasped.

Then, in a fit of anger I hadn't seen since the day we met, Tien rose from his seat under the *kamidana* and strode forward. His senior students paraded at his side, staying several steps ahead of him for his protection. "Excuse me?!" he roared.

"I hear tale of a Chinese running this operation. I want a bout with him. At my school, we don't take well to the Chinese dishing out lessons in our town."

"*Sensei*," started his head student.

"Step back. Now." His voice was beyond dour. The student, as if pulled by a puppeteer, stepped back, leaving Tien at the front of his group. "Anyone who marches into my school, unannounced and spreading hate, will face *my* wrath, not my students'. I take it as a direct challenge. I don't fear losing face in defeat."

"Good. Good." The challenger gleamed through gnarly teeth. "A contest then!"

Tien's face loosened. He was befuddled.

"I challenge you to a match at the center of town. Let all who wish to see come and witness. No holds barred. One on one, so I can show to everyone that the Japanese are superior."

I could sense the rage stewing in Tien's heart. Never had he been berated for his Chinese heritage; out of nowhere, this low life storms into his *dojo* demanding a fight. How Tien held himself back has baffled me to this day.

"I accept your challenge. Under one condition."

The man scoffed. "Name it."

"Shut down your school. For good. And vacate town."

The man's smirk lowered into a slant.

"If I lose, I shall do the same."

My heart sank straightaway. He just put the institution on the line for this raucous clown.

"And what are we to do if you somehow lose?" I interrogated him after the thirty men had left.

"Remember what you taught me those years ago? How looking into your past can bring you wisdom you might have missed?"

I nodded, unsure of where he was getting at.

"Then you have nothing to fear."

He left the room, leaving me standing there on the mat, my hand to my forehead, not able to foresee how this adventure would play out.

∽

The end of the week came quickly. Flyers were strewed about the town, hanging on everything from doors to fence posts, fruit stands to shop windows. On each was a calligraphy of the rival school, its owner, a description of the challenge to preserve national pride for the town, and when and where the challenge was to be held.

"Sundown at the courtyard," Tien whispered to himself, as he had been doing a lot of lately. I couldn't tell if he was nervous. He had never been nervous about any sort of trial, and by the looks of his opponent, I ventured to estimate Tien would have no trouble defeating the brazen punk.

His students each approached him the night of the event before he left from the *dojo*, where he sat beneath the *kamidana* and meditated, preparing himself. They each offered their thanks for everything he had done for them, for his wisdom when it came to matters of combat and life. Some even offered him gifts of *sake* and treats, which I found odd; it wasn't as though he was sick, dying or leaving. Not yet anyway.

Tien dressed in his finest clothes. Two of his students opened the main doors for him, where he looked out to see townsfolk lining the streets, some looking in awe, others apparently sizing him up.

He walked down the boulevard, never once looking at anyone on the side. His focus was certain, his mind at ease but still attentive toward his impending task.

Twilight was beginning. The last of daylight hid away behind the town. Ahead of him was the makeshift arena, a carved-out piece of ground outlined by onlookers. Atop it was grass, flat, dry and plain. Seated on a stool and surrounded by his students was the challenger, still dressed in black and red, but this time in only a sleeveless cotton shirt and workout shorts. He was barefoot, revealing the hardened calluses on his toes, which were oddly shaped from years of abuse. Possibly from repeated striking, possibly from being stomped on, broken and re-broken, but that was neither here nor there.

Tien entered the arena, his students backing him. One of them removed the ornate vest from his shoulders. Another graciously took the tattered *obi* into his hands. He began to loosen himself up, moving his joints around, revealing his impressive flexibility.

The spectators began to chatter amongst themselves, sharing their thoughts about who stood the better chance, who would make the finishing strike, who their bets rested on. None of this deterred Tien in the least. His gaze was strictly fixed upon his enemy.

"Ladies and gentlemen! A match for the ages! To my left, the *dojo-cho* of the Red Dragon Academy, 'The Imperial Beast' Master Saito Yamanaka!" A thunderous applause erupted throughout the courtyard. Claps, squeals and whistles sounded around, filling my ears to the point I couldn't hear the announcer anymore as he continued.

"To my right, the …-*cho* of the … Path School, 'The Devil of the … Valley,' Master Tien!" Another ring of applause exploded throughout the courtyard.

I looked around at the crowd and saw faces I didn't recognize. That's when it became clear that the cheers weren't from the people who knew Tien or his school or his students; the applause came from the folks who simply wanted to see these two fight. They didn't *really* have any favor toward the one they cheered for.

"Ladies and gentlemen, as agreed upon by the two contenders, this match is a No Holds Barred bout. Anything goes. It is over when one party concedes or is unable to continue fighting." The audience roared again. "Gentlemen," the announcer shouted over the commotion, pointing his hands at each of them, "Step forward."

Saito rose from his stool, which was promptly taken and handed off into the audience by another student. He and Tien approached the announcer.

Saito was almost bouncing on his toes, rolling his shoulders and cracking his neck. Tien stood completely still, his narrow eyes trained on Saito.

"Are you ready?!" Another audience cheer. They both nodded their assent. "Assume your positions."

Saito raised his fists up to his face. He tucked his chin tight to his chest.

Tien raised both his hands, bladed his body, and kept a fierce look on Saito.

"*Hajime!!*"

∽

The announcer leapt back to the edge of the crowd, which crept closer into the unmarked arena, pushing and driving in their excitement.

Both contenders cautiously inched closer to one another: Saito elusively bobbed left and right while Tien shuffled his feet softly, gaining more ground one little bit at a time.

Saito threw out random jabs in Tien's direction to keep him from entering his space.

When I looked to see Tien's reaction, I was not surprised that all he did was smirk at the man. His attempts to get Tien to react were fruitless.

Several moments had gone by of just the two sizing each other up. Dull to many of the untrained onlookers but critical to those who knew that both were playing on the edge of the other's range, analyzing for weak points and openings.

Unfortunately, Saito managed the first move, jumping forward as Tien was planting a foot. His fists fired twice as fast as before. Tien scuttled backward, his arms high shielding the incoming strikes. I counted at least ten hits loosed in that time, each one pounding into Tien's two forearms.

Saito broke the connection, pushing back to catch his breath. Tien peeked over his fists; I was surprised to see he was panting a little himself.

Had Tien underestimated Saito's ability? No, Tien is too wise for that, was the answer I offered myself. *Of course, he wouldn't. He knows so little of his style and training method. He wouldn't take it easy on this foe.*

Saito looked ready once more. He bobbed his head side to

side, slipping invisible punches.

Tien moved forward again, reclaiming the ground he had lost. Trying to catch Saito off his own rhythm, he struck swiftly with his own left jab.

Saito managed to flinch out of the way.

As quickly as Tien realized his punch was fruitless, he swung his right leg up and stomped toward Saito's chest.

Saito caught glimpse of the attack and rotated his body, letting the heated foot cruise by.

It was a bad place for Tien; now his back faced Saito, who seized the opportunity, wrapping his arm around Tien's neck and settling in for a choke. The look of triumph was already radiating from his face.

Then, like setting off a spring-loaded trap, Saito was airborne. Tien thrust him effortlessly over his shoulder. Like a bag of wet cement, Saito crashed into the ground; his arm went limp and unwound from Tien's neck.

The crowd gasped and jeered, applauding the genius string of techniques that played out: Tien was able to recognize and adapt to each changing condition at full speed, unrehearsed, and then land a critical move just as his opponent believed he had him in his clutches.

Tien stood up and stepped away from Saito after a few seconds of patient observation, thinking the drop had to be enough to finish the match.

To all our surprise, the limp limbs of his adversary reanimated, flexing and folding. Saito suddenly tensed back up, molded his body into a muscular lump and rolled toward Tien, quickly extending his legs and kicking them skyward into the center of Tien's chest, blowing him off both his feet.

I saw it in slow motion; the concussive impact radiating throughout his torso, the strength in Tien's legs giving out, his jaw dropping open as all the air in his lungs erupted outward. I make no reservations in saying I thought Tien was done for, his school was done for, our reputation was done for.

But as his flaccid body hit the ground, there wasn't the *splat* sound I anticipated hearing. Instead, there was a light patter. His body didn't deaden to a stop. It kept moving, folding, contorting. Tien recovered with his own roll, smoothly landing with one knee down and his right hand in his pocket.

Saito, back on his feet and looking eager to continue, was confused for a moment by the stance. "Don't kneel to me until *after* I've beaten you," he declared.

Onlookers chuckled, quickly turning their gaze to Tien for his reaction.

Tien, astoundingly stoic and unaffected by the powerful kick to his chest, merely rested there, his focus unbroken.

Annoyed by his opponent's silence, Saito pressed in once more, fists up, feet tapping the ground like he was walking on hot coals.

Now. He pulled a pile of rubber training *shuriken* from his *gi* and tossed them, one by one, toward Saito's eyes. The spin he put on the flying stars was so fast that the four expansive points blurred together to look like a singular floating disk.

Saito, blinded by his own hands shielding his face from the small pointed stars, called out ferociously, "Cut that out! This is a fight! You're going against the rules!"

Some of the onlookers *booed* him:

"Don't complain about rule breaking, loser!"

"You gonna let a few rubber stars fluster you?"

The announcer shouted from the sidelines, "No holds barred. Weapons are not forbidden."

As Saito and the announcer shouted back and forth at one another, Tien had risen to both feet, still firing his shots in broken rhythm, moving ever closer to his opponent. Each time Saito lowered his hands to see, Tien shot another.

Once out of ammunition, Tien found himself within striking range of Saito; he threw a sharp lateral kick to the top of his left leg, causing Saito to buckle down and turn.

"*Ahh!*" he screamed instinctively, reaching down for the injured muscle, but Saito resolved to bring it back up and finish the job; he swung a left hook for Tien, who blocked it in time, causing Saito's arm to ricochet off from the sturdy tree trunk that was Tien's right forearm.

Both men exchanged dozens of punches over the next half-minute. They let out all they had left.

Even amid the flurry, I saw snapshots of winces on both players' faces. What was harder to see was each attack that caused them, for both men's recoil and follow-ups were just as quick as the strikes themselves.

Ahh! I heard a distinct yelp from the center of the scene. Tien jerked back and broke the connection with Saito, clasping the side of his throat, making inhuman huffing noises.

Saito bounced closer, the leer on his face gleaming now for

the audience to see. Spectators cheered loudly at the sight of Saito still moving energetically while the pained Tien got lost in the clatter.

I saw him peer swiftly to his sides, watching several of the spectators sounding in his opponent's favor. He looked back through half closed eyes and a furrowing brow. He removed his hand from his throat to reveal a distinct red splotch where Saito's fist made an impression.

The crowd suddenly quieted. Even Saito quit his aggravating bobbing. I then turned my gaze to Tien, who stood there, arms at his sides, fists clenched, his arm muscles glistening with sweat under the final glimmer of sunlight, and veins pulsing from his muscles. It was now quiet enough to hear him puffing fumes from his nose.

He raised his arms up, aiming his front fingers for Saito like a sharpened sword and hiding his right fist behind his front elbow. He set his left foot out farther ahead aiming his toes now right through the center of Saito's body. The look was a look I hadn't witnessed in all my time traveling with Tien; his chin was lowered, his stare darted out from right under the bridge of his brow. The feeling, the attitude he was sending off bled over the crowd. The feeling of tactical destruction, the only words I can attribute to it that might do it any justice. He was so ready and so patient and on the edge of his seat. He was at once inviting Saito to attack him and primed to pounce.

Saito, taken aback by this eerie air that constricted the arena, shook his head slightly, trying to push away the sensation. He lifted his heels and pressed in firmly with the balls of his feet. Locked and ready, he kicked off and sprinted headfirst at Tien.

Saito cocked his right elbow back, opened his mouth and let out a guttural cry, concentrating all his fury into this one conclusive hit.

Wince! Puff! Crumple! Saito's head reeled forward along with his fist, which had gone completely limp. His shoulders pitched forward next in the chain of agony. Tien's front foot was pressing into Saito's lower abdomen; a ripple passed through Saito's skin that traveled all the way to his chest. Tien could feel all the life leaving Saito's muscles.

To be sure Saito did not try to regroup, he flung his foot down behind himself and used his hidden fist to strike the side of Saito's neck. The impact flung Saito's already lax body from where it stood, crumpling him to the ground.

The spectators stood motionless; I looked around and saw their stares of disbelief pouring into the arena. The air had completely changed. I looked back at Tien. He stood there in his position, looking down at his opponent, not yet acting as though the fight was over, but discerning what may come next.

It became quite clear after several moments that Saito was not about to stand back up. His body quivered. His eyes stayed closed, pinched tightly in an effort not to shriek out in pain.

The announcer, numb as well, with his hands outstretched holding back several of the watchers, momentarily forgot his duty. He snapped back to it after blinking a few times, then jumped forward into the arena shouting, "Saito is unable to continue. The winner is Master Tien, the Devil of the Northern

Valley!"

The applause was so outrageous that birds in the trees fled in every direction, filling the sky above us.

I looked to Tien; his muscles finally loosened up after the announcer declared him the winner. He lowered his arms and, as it appeared, for I could no longer hear, sighed heavily. He closed his eyes and perked up one side of his mouth, smirking triumphantly.

$\backsim$

Dozens of people surrounded Tien while he sat at his table trying to indulge in his refreshing beverage. They sounded more like barks, the way they were all trying to gain his attention. He didn't talk back though, didn't wish to recount the tale and subvert the sanctity of the event with his own personal interpretations. *The fight was what it was.*

When it grew so late that his excited fans turned in for the night, Tien, myself and his students followed the long road back to the *dojo*. It was then that Tien finally opened up about the match.

"I found, in those final moments, that the key was to remain patient: invite his attack, give him one chance to strike me down. Then, after he realized he failed—" There was a laugh among the men. "—strike him down instead." Tien said these words so effortlessly, so imperturbably, I couldn't help but shudder for a moment.

I thought about what he said, put myself in his shoes, rendered a scene where I tried to do what he had done, and quickly came to realize that under that amount of stress, in that unusual condition, having onlookers all around, not one of them assisting me, and *also* having something as precious on the line… no way could I do that. No way.

"You should start training then," Tien told me plainly when we sat down inside the dimly lit *dojo*. "Any person from any profession can use these strategies in their work and in their lives."

"How could it help a master writer?" I implored.

"Firstly, don't separate the two. Think instead of the martial art as something that bleeds into and feeds your other passions. If one tries to juxtapose a martial strategy with something else, all they will get in the end is some crude imitation of one or the other. By letting the martial art *become* you, it will seep into your work. What did you learn from my fight today? About me and my tactic?"

"Patience."

"Does not a writer need to have embodied the character of a patient sage to be able to write *as* him instead of *about* him?" I began to see his point. "Think of actors on a stage. They can *pretend* tears, but where is the soul behind it that the audience desires to connect with, to be enthralled by and drawn into?

"A man who calls himself a martial artist who has only ever studied the strikes and the throws and the locks, is not a martial artist; he is a fighter. And there are great fighters, scary fighters. But they are not artists.

"An artist is someone who cultivates himself and aspires to

bring himself to the closest form of perfection he can in his limited time here in this world. It's such a general characterization, I know, but it's because the realm we speak of is so vast; I feel it would take a lifetime to explain—"

"Because it takes a lifetime to explore," I finished.

Tien nodded. I could see that behind his eyes he was trying to piece together all the things he could to try to illuminate for me what he was trying to express, but when that became too much, he let out a soft exhale, and simply finished with: "It is okay if you do not understand."

『...終 』

Sensei took one final glance at the words. He reverently contemplated them. His fingers caressed the leather cover resting in his fingertips. Then, he flipped the page and saw a message scrawled in a heavier ink. It was written erratically across the lower half of the page:

To my dear friend,

In my last days, I wanted to give you the final draft of our journey together, a copy with a grand conclusion to set in stone the impact that our time together has had on me. Even though I will no longer be with you, I hope my words will one day help to rejuvenate your exhausted spirit whenever you may need them. Pray your own wisdom will pull you from the pits of any slump you find yourself in. Here's to a joyous life, my friend. Oh, and I hope you don't mind the torn-out pages at the front. I thought it suited the aesthetic.

-Kokoro, 1978

Underneath the message, a crimson stamp emblazoned Kokoro's family seal overtop the signature:

謙信

Sensei removed his hand from the leather binding and wiped his finger underneath his eye, catching a single tear. He wiped it along his shirt, then flipped through the remaining blank pages until they had all folded over. Stuffed in a pocket in the back of the book was a set of small, old black-and-white photographs. He pulled them from their nest, closed the cover and placed them atop the journal.

Imaged on the top photo was a group of people standing beneath a *kamidana*, all dressed in their white training *gi*. *Sensei* scanned the faces of all the students, recognizing each and every one. Though many had gone on to pursue other things over the years, he recounted their time in that training hall: bowing in together, training hard, seeking that perfection explained to him by his own teachers.

Sensei's eyes stopped on the final two fellows in the image who sat on the floor in front of the group. One was a slender individual with fair hair and a gleaming grin. The man next to him was a shorter individual with narrow eyes, whose smile was thin and whose neck sported a massive bruise on its side. *Sensei* chuckled and sniffed at the same time, feeling the top of the photo paper, then raising his hand to feel his aged neck. "Oh, what time does to us, eh, Kokoro?"

He flipped the photograph over. In thin ink, a title and date were written down the side:

Warrior's Path School Student Body
Day After "Saito's Defeat"
Summer 1962

"Kokoro, once again, you've given me strength." *Sensei* slid the photos back into their pocket, closed and bound the cover of the journal and placed it back into the drawer of his paltry desk.

He flipped the switch to the *samurai* desk lamp, strode to the door, turned off the overhead lights, and left the room, reassured about what he would do next.

∽

Two tense weeks had passed. *Sensei* sat again with Owen and Bill at the same table with the same drinks across from the same Mr. Stewart, whose anticipatory gaze loomed over them. "Thanks for meeting again, gentlemen," he began drolly. "What have you all decided about my offer?"

Sensei rolled his shoulders around, adjusting himself in the stony coffee shop seat. He took a breath. "We sincerely thank you for all the work you've put into your proposal, Mr. Stewart," *sensei* said curtly, "and, at this time, we do *not* wish to take on any of your organization's services."

Mr. Stewart's keen smile suddenly twisted with an obvious fury. His eyes grew cold. "Well," he began, "is there anything in my proposal we might be able to negoc—"

Sensei cut him off of his crooked banter. "I've taken the last two weeks to look back at what it was that got me to this point. I've been in this business for some time, Mr. Stewart, no doubt longer than you've been alive. I've traveled the world over: East Asia, the Pacific isles, the Mediterranean. I've had the fortune of training with legends from various arts so that I may improve myself, both as an artist and as a human, and then share that knowledge with my students, the passionate men and women who set aside leisure, safety, sometimes sanity," he said with a chuckle.

Mr. Stewart was not amused by the gag.

Where *sensei* would usually clear his throat and truck on, he merely closed his mouth and continued to throw Mr. Stewart an unpretentious look that dug into his eyes.

Owen and Bill felt this tension, like the force of good trying to rebound the force of evil. They noticed that *sensei* was unmoved, so he continued, "What I am getting at, Mr. Stewart, is that there is a strong change in the times between my generation and yours."

Owen and Bill turned their heads to their teacher. *Surely, he can't mean us*, they thought.

"I look around and see all these young men and women paying these memberships to these schools and training to get strong – admirable, yes, and part of the journey, certainly – but then they take their skill and flaunt it around, looking for these endorsements and fighting over these belts and arguing on the television, backhanding their rivals in these press interviews. What are they promoting, Mr. Stewart? I was never brought up by my teachers in that way. This art, and many others, they are meant to keep peace and promote self-mastery, but all this keeps getting clouded and defiled.

"What you are proposing, Mr. Stewart, is just another way to buy my school into that culture. But as a teacher, I have an obligation to spread the wisdom I've cultivated over decades. I can never turn back on that if it goes against the principles that laid the groundwork for my school and my students."

Owen and Bill lowered their heads at their *sensei's* words.

Sensei rose from his seat and looked down at Mr. Stewart, who clearly wasn't moved by *sensei's* diatribe. "That is my final decision. Again, thank you for all you've done. It has truly helped me." *Sensei* gave a short bow to the cross man on the other side of the table, then walked off.

Owen stood and followed his teacher. Bill reached his hand across to shake Mr. Stewart's, but the man remained still, a glassy stare shooting back, his hands unmoving; Bill then rose hesitantly and walked away.

"I suppose, you have another plan, *sensei?*" Owen asked him nervously.

"We will formulate one together, Owen. We mustn't forget where *our* values lie. I haven't come all this way over the years to be shut out by the corrupted taste of today's 'martial arts.' We must find a way to inspire those on the outside to come seek out their own self-mastery and keep alive what true martial arts stand for."

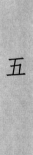

五

THE UNNAMED MASTER AND
THE MAPLE BRANCH

無名の達人とメープルの枝

The full moon hung low, creeping through the thick autumn clouds. Several students knelt down in the shadows of the pine trees and observed the open hilly field as their fellow junior classmates – tonight, their competition – snuck across the soft ground.

The three older students rocked this way and that as their old knees began to ache from crouching for so long. In the smallest of whispers, one of the three asked, "Can't we just go get them ourselves?"

The faintest *shhh* fell from his comrade's mouth.

The man rolled his eyes.

"Stay focused," the third added through his pinched lips.

"They're never going to find us at this rate. What

if we draw their attention this way, you know, help speed things along?"

"That's not the point, Dan. This is the young ones' task. Let them figure it out," said the second in her high voice.

"I don't want to be here all night, Mariel."

"Do you want *sensei* to fail us for being impatient? Really? You've been doing this how long?" Walter rebutted irately.

"It's not about passing or failing. It's about surviving," said a voice from behind the three, who all stirred atop the pine needles turning to face the obscured figure. Walter and Dan both gasped. Mariel was able to keep quiet; she looked back out to the field to see if their targets heard the commotion.

"Is that you, *sensei*?" asked Dan, dubiously.

"Of course, it's me. I could see you three plain as day." Each pouted in learning that their expertly executed concealing strategy had been thwarted without them ever noticing. "And one more thing: as senior instructors, I'd expect you to never take away an opportunity for a student to learn something. Trying to lure them in on a scouting assignment? Dan, *tsk tsk*," he whispered with a laugh. "At least you didn't give yourselves away."

Sensei looked out to the field and noticed the three novices heading in the opposite direction; he sighed. Dan looked at him with edginess. "Just two more minutes," *sensei* asserted.

∽

The seven of them convened at the top of the tallest hill. The moonlight came and went erratically as the clouds overhead began to speed around.

"So, your team went well off course," *sensei* began to say to the three younger students, "There's two explanations for it. The first: you overlooked critical evidence. The second: your targets were just too skilled to leave traces behind."

Was that a compliment? The instructors pondered, grinning nonetheless.

"That was not the case this round, however."

Just like that, their poise was crushed.

"This shouldn't dishearten any of you, though. Mistakes are made. That's what training is for. We work out all the possible outcomes, eliminate the less favorable ones, so when it comes time for action, we do the right thing. We don't get stuck in a trap we set for ourselves."

Even in the fainting moonlight, *sensei* saw his pupils nodding their heads as they considered his wisdom.

"And such training as we've done tonight is not something you can learn in one try. Constant practice, changing the conditions, all these things are part of the journey." He turned to the three instructors. "How long did it take you to feel comfortable with getting in close to an opponent, Mariel?"

Her eyes widened, followed by her mouth. She shifted her weight, thinking for a moment. "Well, I'm still working on that," Dan and Walter also shook their heads, agreeing, "but it was definitely about three years before it really started to stick, to become a part of how I move." The three younger students listened to her attentively.

"Would it have served you any good if your first teachers

pushed the process along by feeding you your take-downs instead of you working for them?"

"No, it would have been a great disservice."

"That is what we, as instructors, are there to do. We guide
the student along. We've been down that part of the road before. We can give the student the directions, but what kind
of journey is it if we hold their hand the whole way through?
Meaningless, meaningless," *sensei* repeated adamantly. "This art
is about the journey. No one is rushing you. Understanding
comes in time."

『昔々...』

There is a legend from the old ascetics of the mountains of
Japan shared with the youngest of students to teach them
the importance of persistence and guiding others down the path
of warriorship.

On a mountain peak stood a *tengu* in the springtime of his
years. He looked over the top of the mountain and saw the vast-
ness of the long valley, raging rivers, and glossy hillsides below.
In his hand, he held a long *bokken*. Its handle was stained of
oils from the young *tengu's* grip.

He trained with this *bokken* every day for hours at a time.
He would find bamboo reeds as thick as his arm and strike at
them tirelessly to improve his skill. He used large leaves from
the maples that blew in the winds and cut at them for target
practice. Every day, he became a little bit stronger; his rigorous
regimen left him sore each morning, but he learned to fight

through the aches and continued to improve.

In his martial tradition, the eldest *tengu* of his mountain clan presented those who reached a certain level in their training a blade that unlocked a mystical ability, one that reflected the prowess of the warrior's fighting spirit.

In the years the young *tengu* had been training, he had seen his *senpai* be awarded their numinous blades. They would stretch their wings and soar the air currents through the mountain valley, invoking the power of their sharpened weapons.

One of his *senpai* could harness lightning from the tip of his sword. Another's blade was endowed with the power to cast a cloak of clouds around himself to hide from the sight of his enemies. Even another could turn his blade into molten steel and reshape it into any weapon he needed during a battle.

The young *tengu* looked on enthusiastically as his *senpai* boasted the prize of their tough training. As the years continued, more and more of his fellows reached this level and were awarded their lavish armament.

Then came the days his *kohai* began receiving their blades as well. As happy and supportive as he tried to be, he felt a pain of jealousy in his gut.

The young *tengu* did not understand. His hands were raw from training with his *bokken* tirelessly every day. The tan wood of the long end was clearly bright and splintered while the handle featured a darker blemished tinge. Surely his masters could see the result of his training.

Being around them all with their gaudy weapons began to make him twinge. A fire lit in him every time someone new unlocked their hidden power. This only made him train harder and more recklessly, thrashing his bamboo targets and swinging flagrantly at the maple leaves.

∽

Several days had passed. The young *tengu* was uncommonly sorer from his wild training, so he decided to rest one afternoon down in a town in the center of the valley. From a high tree, he looked down at the people, walking through the streets, their attention elsewhere.

Out of the crowd, a young girl, maybe seven years of age, stood in front of a small house, its living quarters on the top floor and a square space with a hardwood floor on the bottom. The young *tengu* was curious as to what caught the little girl's attention, so he leapt from the tree branches, transformed into a sparkling silver cat, and landed on his feet. He walked over to the girl, curled himself around her legs and sat, looking in through the open door.

The empty space was a makeshift *dojo*. On the floor inside were six men with *bokken* practicing forms. Their cuts and blocks looked strong and deliberate, and their parries were smooth and swift. Sweat bounced from their skin with each of their motions. They shouted in time with their strikes, attacking their partners with exacting force.

The cat lifted his head to see the look on the little girl's face. Her eyes lit up like two stars. She was awed by their power, focus and spirit.

Yelp! The cat cried out. The little girl stepped on his tail as she was tugged by the hand of her father, who insisted they keep moving. The girl strained her free hand, pointing wildly at the *dojo*.

Her father, nonetheless amused, shook his head definitively, then tugged again on his daughter's hand, escorting her away.

The cat saw the face of the girl sink from its look of hopeful wonder. He leapt back into the trees and thought to himself, *everyone with the righteous heart deserves the chance to train.*

∽

The next day, after meditating under the large maple at the top of the hallowed mountain, the young *tengu* picked up his *bokken* from the ground, turned to a branch of the tree and swung with all his might. The branch snapped cleanly away from the rest of the trunk. He then took his *bokken* and stripped away the excess stems, smoothing it down to fit comfortably in his grip.

With the two weapons in hand, he spread his wings and jumped from the peak, gliding down into the town.

He drifted for a while, eyeing the homes below, looking for the little girl. He spotted her in her backyard, despondently fiddling with a doll in the garden next to a shrine.

The doll was dressed in a sapphire *kimono* and sporting long silky hair. Its dress was so tight to its torso, the legs were inflexible. The girl moved the doll's arms around, imitating the actions of the *budōka* she had seen in town. She had tied the doll's hair together into a single tail, so it wouldn't get into its own face as it punched in the air.

Out of nowhere, she heard a *thud* in the grass. She looked over her shoulder and found the smoothened maple branch lying behind her. Curiously, she peered around, knowing there were no maples just dropping branches into her family's garden.

Then, she spotted him, the young *tengu* who wore a black *obi*, red shoulder cloth and slate grey *hakama*. He perched his talon feet on the shingles of the roof, squatting low and staring down at the inquisitive girl.

He gestured to the girl to pick it up.

She did. She gripped it in her hands, holding it in just the right places, like it came naturally to her what to do.

The young *tengu* was enthralled. He vaulted from the roof and down into the garden, slowing himself with his outstretched white feathered wings. The little girl didn't recoil. Instead, she stood there, looking up, captivated by the tall beast before her.

The young *tengu* raised his *bokken* over his head, paused for a moment, giving the girl a look of pure focus, then swung down at an invisible target. He did so one more time, then gestured for the girl to try.

She did, mimicking the cut almost unerringly. The young *tengu* was so pleased.

They trained together for another few hours, then decided to part as the sun began to set. The young *tengu* bowed to the girl, who politely bowed in return. He stretched his wings once more and flapped them, ascending steadily until he turned and set a course. With another flap, he darted away toward his mountain home.

The little girl watched her teacher as he flew off into the distance. When she could no longer see him, she looked down at where he last stood. She noticed one of his feathers lying at her feet. She picked it up and held it to the last remaining rays of light. As the sun finished setting and night rained on the garden, the feather evaporated from the girl's grasp.

Just as the young *tengu*, the little girl shut herself away for the night, eager for her next chance to train.

∽

The cycle went on for many years. The young *tengu* would train himself with his trusty *bokken*, now splintered and dented more than ever, then fly down to the town and train with the little girl, whose skills with her maple *bokken* had grown exponentially.

After countless meetings, it was no longer right to call themselves the young *tengu* and little girl. They were both grown now. They sparred with the same intensity as the players in the makeshift *dojo* that the girl had seen long before.

One day, just before the *tengu* was set to voyage into town, he stood at the peak and watched another young warrior receive his mystical blade, which could create copies of the wielder to bewilder his adversaries. The *tengu* looked upon the younger, neither jealous nor upset. Instead, he trained his energies on improving himself and coaching the girl in the ways of the sword. Just as he had once seen the *budōka* from that *dojo* all those

years ago, he was impressed by their mutual skill that came
from working hard together.

They were not worried about anything in their future; they
set themselves firmly in the present, using every moment together to sharpen themselves. The young woman's *bokken* was
finally starting to resemble the *tengu's*: battered, dented, and
stained with sweat and oil. The two were nearly one in terms of
skill and spirit.

∽

One day, amid their sparring, a great wind kicked up, blowing around the tree leaves in the garden and loosening some
shingles on the roof above. The ground quaked as another, larg-
er tengu landed in front of the shrine. He brandished a bright,
polished sword much longer than the two's measly *bokken*.

His name was Kazemon, and his blade had the power to
summon gusts to cut through enemies. He was one of the oldest *tengu* from the mountain and said to be one of the most
formidable.

Kazemon pointed down at the woman who wielded a *bokken* carved from one of the great maples. His crow face cringed
spitefully.

The smaller *tengu* stepped forward and explained how he
had taken on this woman as a student some time before, and
how he fashioned the *bokken* from the great maple tree so it
would last a long time and help her grow stronger.

Kazemon had heard enough. He thrust his large arm between them, kicking up a blast of cold, sharp air. The *tengu*, screaming through the wind, rebutted that he should see the skill the young woman had accrued over the years.

Kazemon didn't care if it was the woman's first day. He was enraged to the point he didn't pause and think. He swung his blade at the woman intending to cut her down. Together, the *tengu* and woman held their weapons out like a cross and blocked Kazemon's cut, stopping it in its tracks.

The giant Kazemon wound up again and, with even more power, slashed down, knowing this time he would decimate both of their *bokken*.

The teacher and pupil quickly split up and ran along Kazemon's sides.

Kazemon's strike did not stop. His blade crashed into the garden floor. Wind burst out at his left and right, cleanly slicing the blades of grass and blowing the pieces up into the air.

As the two came in with a strike of their own, Kazemon flapped his enormous wings and flew up passed the roof of the house. Circling the garden, Kazemon looked down to observe the movements of his prey. He planned on striking the traitorous *tengu* first, so he curled in his wings and dove down like a bomb, leading with his glistening sword.

The *tengu* jumped and flipped, twirling his *bokken* around his body, and as Kazemon unfurled his wings to set course upward again, the *bokken* struck down atop his head.

Kazemon crashed, skidding along the ground and thudding into the shrine.

The woman ran forward and jumped up just as Kazemon

lifted his large head. She brought her weapon down onto Kazemon's birdlike skull. The concussive strike echoed like a thunderclap, but it was not enough to down him.

Kazemon rattled his head around, then swiped again with his arm. Another gust blew toward the two, knocking them both down to their seat. Kazemon stood, raising his blade. Seeing the two stuck on the ground next to one another, he swung decisively one last time.

The two gripped their *bokken* tightly, rightfully scared beyond comprehension. Nothing would be able to save them now.

Just then, they felt a strange vibration in their wooden weapons. A strange blue glow radiated along the surface of the maple wood, then, like jagged waves in a sea storm, coursed up the length of the weapon.

Together, they raised their *bokken* and made a cut right on the path of Kazemon's sword. For the briefest of moments, there was a sharp *clang!* The steel of the sword hitting the maple wood let off a ring that pierced all of their ears. A burst of air erupted around them, popping the screens of the windows. All three looked up to see the commotion. The portals were vacant except for the shades now flapping out of them like ghosts dancing in the breeze.

Then, without warning, Kazemon's blade also began to reverberate, and not in a way he ever noticed before. They all brought their gaze down to the sight. The duo noticed Kazemon's hand begin to quiver violently. They pressed their weapons in with one… final… thrust.

Kazemon's steel chipped… then cracked… then snapped…

from the sharp end to the dull. The cold piece of steel flew to the other end of the garden, glimmering in the light as it spun wildly.

The air... fell still.

The two partners knelt there, panting. Their grip was still firm. The blue aura slowly faded away.

Kazemon, looking first at his broken weapon and then at the two before him, stepped away slowly. Without a word, knowingly defeated, he flew straight up into the sky, leaving the worthless broken steel behind.

The young woman asked how it was possible that their *bokken* could possibly dismantle Kazemon's blade, to which the *tengu* answered: I do not know.

∽

The next day, the story spread of how the young *tengu*, aided by a human, had defeated Kazemon, one of the elite warriors of the hallowed mountain. He was summoned forward before the masters to be awarded his own blade of power. He accepted it graciously.

The masters told him that his blade granted him the power of 'severance,' not only able to cut through injustices, as with Kazemon's sword, but also sacrifice a piece of his own power to feed his allies extra needed strength. That was the power he had hidden within him all along. He invoked the power in his friend and pupil when she needed it most.

He was given the name Danzo, and with his new blade in

hand, he celebrated his triumph with all the other *tengu* on the mountain.

∽

The young woman felt something majestic riding the winds that day. There was a gentleness, a peace with every breath she took.

A shadow briefly disrupted her vision, then a feather fell before her and landed at her feet. She turned to see her friend, who was now wearing a crimson *obi*. Tucked within the fabric was a sheathed sword, and tied around it on the other hip was a leather satchel.

He held another long object in his hands wrapped in a forest green cloth. Danzo held out the item to his friend.

She unfolded the end of the cloth, which revealed a darkly stained handle. She took a hold of it and pulled it free from its wrap. The old *bokken* vibrated in her hand.

Danzo explained that now she was responsible for the same power: the power to cut through injustice. It was a power few could wield responsibly, but knowing of how the young woman displayed her power before and radiated the same spirit as her teacher, he could entrust this human with his old weapon.

The legend concludes that Danzo soared off into the skies, never returning again, but as he sailed away, the breeze from his feathered wings blew off all the leaves from the garden trees.

Winter came early to the young woman's town, along with it a parade of villainous visitors, but armed with her and Danzo's strength, she became the town's trusted guardian and led it to a peaceful spring.

『...終 』

*S*ensei stood for a moment underneath the fast-moving clouds looking at his students, the three young and the three old. A flood of memories rushed through his aged mind: his first *sensei* taking him on as a pupil, his first public match, opening his school, passing on the instructor role to his first batch of senior students. Though he stood stoically before them, the torrent of emotions stirred his insides.

After taking a moment to gather himself, he offered one final piece of wisdom. "Your time training with friends on the same path is the real secret to excelling in the mystical endeavor that is martial arts. Never forget that. You need each other, and you need to keep spreading this art about. What good does it do to see our art die? You are the protectors. You are the ones who will change the world."

エピローグ 滝

EPILOGUE

THE CASCADE

The current was inhospitable that day. They weren't going to make the journey. It was far too risky. The entire week before was nothing but a monsoon in the mountains, and all the rainwater was gathering into the stream. In all the years we had made this hike, never had Mother Nature been this unforgiving.

It has always been a rite of passage: when you take a new step in your training, you make the hike to the bottom. You confront your fear, you face the elements, you test yourself against everything outside of your control to see if your spirit really is strong enough.

I had trekked the long winding trail for many years, as had Tien. This time was to be our first with new advancing students. But for their safety, we made them stay behind.

An odd double standard: teachers, acting like parents, saying, "No, you mustn't. Now wait here while we do." I could
see how they'd be angry if they knew we journeyed down the
dangerous trails without them.

But there was no point in arguing: what was done was done.

We arrived at the bottom after the three-mile hike down the
six tumultuous switchbacks. We could hear the water echoing
up the trail, pounding away at the boulders below. The volume
of water this year was unlike any we'd ever witnessed.

But I wasn't scared. I couldn't be.

Making my way to this rare site tucked away in the mountains, deluging myself underneath a waterfall, succumbing to
forces unreproducible anywhere else.

The first time, it's scary: walking atop the large slick mossy
boulders, sliding your way down the slope to the entrance of
the cave. Not like any other cave, not some gap in a stone wall.
This cave was crafted from collapsing boulders having tumbled
down from hundreds of feet up, coming to a stop, miraculously
forming a small passageway down into the lower level of the
falls.

Once inside, you stand alone. Around you are three damp
sides of giant colorless stone. Mist sprays around the entire
passage. The fourth side is nothing but a wall of water. If the
weather is right, the sun smiles down on you through the ever-
flowing curtain, brightening your *gi* and reflecting your sense of
joy and pride. You think to yourself, *I made it to the final step,
the final test.*

You grab the vines that dangle down from above, find your

footing, then step into the cascade. Your head dips down into the little pocket of air, and you gasp for breath as the water beats your back, forcing that same air right back out. If you aren't ready, it feels as though you're suffocating. Your heart races. Your spirit quakes.

But that is the test. Mastering nature by mastering yourself. It took several years and several trials before I started to get the hang of it. Now, I can step in and last for minutes, standing firm under the falls, thinking about the last year of training, of writing, of the adventures I'd had.

When the time feels right, I step back out from under the water and watch as it courses on.

The monster that was this year's falls was a beast that outmatched all others. The sun wasn't strong enough to cut through the uncharacteristic smoke gray clouds. A haze sailed overhead, almost concealing us from the rest of the forest.

Tien was the first to enter in. I stood on top of the boulder, listening to the rushing sounds beneath my feet. When he entered, the tone changed dramatically. I could hear the water beating against his back as it gushed down the front of the cave. He let out a roar as he powered against it. The second holler was not as strong as the first, and the third was simply cut short. Then the sound of rushing water became steady again.

Tien climbed back up through the stone portal; I reached my hand down to hoist him up the rest of the way. He wore a rare grimace when I looked at him. "It's rough," he muttered, still struggling for air.

"Is it worth it?" I asked.

Without hesitating, he vigorously nodded his head. Beads of water sprung from his hair and struck me on the face. "It's worth it."

I sighed one last time, then removed my shirt and shoes. I stepped into the cave. I felt the slippery spots where Tien had climbed back up. I grabbed ahold of a stray vine that was growing down into the passageway, hoping it'd give me some support, but it was young and fragile; it snapped free almost instantly. So, with great care, I stepped one hand and one foot at a time until I made it to the bottom.

On the flat base of the cave, I looked around, seeing the cave walls completely drenched and hearing the echoes pound around the space. I turned and faced the wall of water that crashed down as though from a giant burst pipe.

I reached a hand into the torrent. The droplets battered my skin as they fell faster than gravity. Plunging myself was going to hurt, I could tell. But Tien had done it, and he trained me, so there was no way I could let it defeat me.

I stepped one leg forward under the falls. Yes, it stung. A combination of the chilling sensation and the physical pounding, but now that I had taken my first step through, there was no sense in turning back.

In a single motion, I dove in. My head was quickly concussed, forced forward; my neck muscles strained to keep it up. My shoulders, too, were being forced down. It was as though chains were hooked to them, and the chains were being yanked down beneath me by the demons of the mountain.

I tried to inhale, but the mist hung in the air, finding its way into my throat. As the pounding persisted, I mustered all I could into one powerful outburst.

ARGH!

It didn't last long. Maybe a second and a half, but I squeezed all the air out from my guts in that one explosive bellow.

I stepped out from under the water, wiped my eyes with my soaked hands, only making it worse, then climbed up the stone steps to the mouth of the cave where a hand reached down and hoisted me up.

"Was it worth it?" Tien gleamed at me, excited now.

I rolled my shoulders and cracked my neck both ways. "It was worth it." I smiled.

We both looked up at the taller section of the waterfall, the twenty-story beast flowing down irreverently into the water pool just upstream from the cave.

I reflected once more on my adventures of that year, the countries I had traveled to in search of new teachers to study from, then cast the memories to the back of my mind. The waterfall had cleansed me in preparation for another year, one which, if nature was foretelling, was going to be rough.

But also foretelling was the way we pushed through it, not giving in to the pressure that tried to suck the air out of us, not stumbling and not backing down.

昭和五十三年吉日

This auspicious day in 1978

謙信

先生の知恵

Sensei's Training Tips

———

一 / Do it because you love it!

二 / Everyone can teach you something you need to learn if you are quiet enough to hear it.

三 / Passion is constant, but training is rhythmic. The body needs time to rest. Don't burn yourself out.

四 / A bundle of sticks is stronger than one stick alone. Keep your friends in mind when it comes to training.

五 / If you aren't frustrated, you aren't any closer to mastery. Let frustration motivate you but not deter you.

語
彙

GLOSSARY

---

arigatō - "thank you"

bo - wooden staff

bokken - wooden sword

budōka - one who studies the Way of the Warrior

daimyō - feudal lord

Danzo - "severance | gain, augment"

dōjō - place of the Way; training hall

dōjō-chō - training hall chief; head of the *dōjō*

gi - training uniform (also called *dōgi*)

hai! - "yes!"

hajime! - "begin!"

hakama - loose trousers with many pleats in the front

hanko - official seal

Jiro - common name of second born male

kamidana - spirit shelf

kanji - Japanese writing using Chinese pictograms

Kazemon - "wind | gate"

kohai - rear generation; junior student

Kurogawa - "black | river"

mukashimukashi - "Once upon a time..."

ninja - person of perseverance

obi - belt

owaru - to end; "The End"

Saburo - common name of third born male

sake - rice wine

samurai - feudal warriors in the service of powerful lords

seiza - "correct | seat"; sitting on your feet

senpai - prior generation; senior student

sensei - one who comes before; teacher

shuriken - "hand | inside | blade"; metal throwing star

tabi - split-toe shoes

Taro - common name of first born male

tatami - mat

tengu - half-bird half-man winged mountain/forest creature

作者について

ABOUT THE AUTHOR

Justin is a black belt practitioner in Stephen K. Hayes' To-Shin Do® martial art. He graduated from the University of North Carolina at Chapel Hill in 2011. He avidly pursues opportunities in the fields of photography, literature, and film production to work in conjunction with his martial arts training.

As of this publication, he is an instructor at Chapel Hill Quest Martial Arts in North Carolina. He became the school's Director of Youth Education in 2013.

CPSIA information can be obtained
at www.ICGtesting.com
Printed in the USA
FFOW03n0325021217
43879566-42883FF

9 780999 689103